# My Secret Fantasies

---

### Joanne Rock

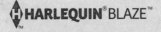
HARLEQUIN® BLAZE™

Recycling programs
for this product may
not exist in your area.

ISBN-13: 978-0-373-79786-8

MY SECRET FANTASIES

Copyright © 2014 by Joanne Rock

Printed in U.S.A.

# ABOUT THE AUTHOR

While working on her master's degree in English literature, Joanne Rock took a break to write a romance novel and quickly realized a good book requires as much time as a master's program itself. She became obsessed with writing the best romance possible, and sixty-some novels later, she hopes readers have enjoyed all the "almost there" attempts. Today, Joanne is a frequent workshop speaker and writing instructor at regional and national writer conferences. She credits much of her success to the generosity of her fellow writers, who are always willing to share insights on the process. More important, she credits her readers with their kind notes and warm encouragement over the years for her joy in the writing journey.

Books by Joanne Rock

For Lisa Manasier,
who made me kale chips while I wrote,
who has encouraged me in more ways than she knows,
and who has always had my back.
I love you like a sister.

# _Prologue_

_"Is anyone there?" Shaelynn called, knocking on the door of the only house she'd seen after hours of walking through the cold, snowy dark. Her snowmobile had died miles from her hotel, crashing nose-first into a frozen stream. She'd lost her cell phone._

_This Colorado getaway had stopped being fun and started being scary when she could no longer feel her toes. She had to get inside and get warm...fast._

_"Hello?" She banged on the door again...._

MY FINGERS HOVERED over the computer keys as I paused to reread what I'd just written. While my fictional heroine shivered in the mountains, I sat in my vacant L.A. apartment. All my worldly possessions were already packed in the SUV, and I was leaving town tomorrow. For tonight, I deserved a fun distraction. Ever since I'd taken it into my head to write a naughty novel, I'd been having a great time with my characters.

The world of steamy fiction was a vast improvement over my job as a struggling actress—a job I'd finally realized didn't suit me one bit. And writing was far, far better than my awful experience on a popular reality series that had made me one of the most gossiped-about women in Los Angeles. Most of all, I had the sense that penning this book would finally heal some demons I'd been running from ever since I'd left home at eighteen. Closure on that dark chapter of my life was long overdue—especially since running from it had only made the past implode.

Drumming my fingers lightly along the keys, I forced those thoughts aside to concentrate on what happened next in the story, while on another screen, I waited for a reply on my instant message regarding a piece of property I wanted to see tomorrow. This business deal could give me the time and freedom to finally write my book. I'd scrimped and saved, living like a pauper, to finance the next phase of my life. Now that I'd won that reality game show series, I finally had enough starter money to get to work on my dreams. And not a minute too soon, given how much grief I'd taken because of the show ever since filming ended three weeks ago. Given how much grief a long-lost boyfriend was trying to create for me.

Shuddering, I turned back to the story.

*"Is anyone home?" Shaelynn called one last time before she trudged through the knee-deep snow, her legs shaking from exhaustion and cold. Maybe she'd have better luck at the back door.*

*Shoving through the negligible barrier of an overgrown boxwood hedge, she peered around the back cor-*

*ner of the cabin. Another exterior light burned, just like
in front. But inside, the place looked completely dark.
Hopelessness threatened to swamp her as she banged
on that door, too.*

*"Help!" she called, her voice echoing in the sharp
cold. "Help!" She backed up a step so she could yell
at the whole house.*

*And rammed right into a low wall.*

*"Oof," she muttered, slipping. She grabbed on to the
structure to keep herself from falling. Only to realize it
wasn't a wall at all. It was a hot tub.*

*Built into the cabin's raised deck, the tub had a thick,
insulated leather covering. A thin trail of steam wafted
from the seam where the cover met the cedar siding.*

*Heat. Warmth. A guarantee of survival.*

*All those things awaited her there beneath that tarp.
Who would call it trespassing when she was at risk of
freezing to death out here?*

*Mind made up, Shaelynn tugged off her coat and un-
buttoned her blouse with stiff, shaking fingers....*

I imagined myself there in the crisp, clear air of the
Rockies, sliding down among the hot jets of an outdoor
spa. It was possible half the fun of this book was the
access it gave me to the kind of life I'd always dreamed
about. A sensuous life full of great sex was something
I'd never quite managed in the real world. Far from it.
I'd dropped a few dress sizes since high school, thinking I'd get over some of my insecurities by changing
the external stuff. No dice. Now I would tackle those

hang-ups through my book, where I could live out a vicarious existence of someone who was hot and sexy.

First fiction. Then real life.

Speaking of which…

*Steam wafted up Shaelynn's cheek like the touch of a phantom lover. After half an hour in the hot tub, she'd finally started to feel warm again. Her toes had quit throbbing. She'd quit jumping at every sound in the woods and had turned the jets on full blast. Now, the heat relaxed her. The pure decadence of being naked beneath the water made her whole body feel deliciously languid.*

*Tilting her neck back on the headrest, she stared up at the stars and breathed deep.*

*Until the sound of a dog barking made her sit up.*

*She listened hard, switching off the pump for the hot tub jets so she could hear better. Had she imagined it?*

*The bark came again. Closer. Followed by the definite crack of twigs and movement of something—something human sized—in the woods nearby.*

*Panic sliced through her as she detected the shadow of a man approaching. Should she sit still and pray he passed? Shout for help even though she was miles from anywhere and her phone was lost in the snow?*

*Before she could decide, the tall, masculine shadow emerged from the trees, scattering soft clouds of fresh powder with each step of his snowshoes. Dear God, what if he lived here?*

*She shook her head. Of course he lived here. Why else would man and dog be making a beeline straight to-*

*ward her? There were no other houses for miles around. If she hadn't been naked, she might have darted out of the tub to hide. But she was most definitely naked and her clothes were on the other side of the small deck.*

*The dog spotted her first, barking like mad and big as a bear.*

*"Rex, heel," the man's deep voice called, quieting the animal before he asked, "Who's there?"*

*Broad, square shoulders took shape in the moonlight, along with a gray canvas coat unbuttoned despite the cold.*

*"Um." Shaelynn cleared her throat, nerves making her sound shaky. "I broke down a couple of miles away. Your light was the only one I saw and when you weren't home..."*

*She trailed off, distracted by the sight of the man as he slowly walked closer, and the glow of the back porch lantern illuminated his features.*

*Hazel eyes. Thick, dark eyebrows. A chiseled, aristocratic face that could be Mediterranean. An arresting face. Strong. Handsome. He huffed out a breath of warm air, the light cloud swirling for a moment until it vanished into the cold.*

*"You needed to warm up," he finished for her, his eyes roaming over the deck where her clothes sat in a pile, then returning to her. Lingering.*

*Her heart beat faster. She swallowed past her dry throat.*

*"I'm sorry. I can go. But I lost my cell phone in the snow and I'm—"*

*"You can use my phone." The man ventured closer.*

*The deck was a few feet off the ground, but the snow-fall put him on even footing with the base of the tub. His eyes locked on hers, stirring something deep inside her. "And my towels."*

*A slow, half smile lifted the corner of his mouth. Maybe she should be afraid. But fear was the last thing she felt as he sauntered up to the side of the spa.*

*Did he know she was nude? She glanced down, grateful she hadn't put the underwater light on. Pulse thrumming wildly, she withdrew her hand from the water, because touching this tall, sexy stranger was definitely not optional. She suddenly craved the feel of him....*

Bing!

The chime of an instant message rang, startling me from Shaelynn's hot tub adventures just when things were about to get interesting. I had to stop to fan myself, visions of the sexy stranger enticing me as much as they affected my heroine.

How come I never met gorgeous strangers who made me melt with a glance? Forcing my thoughts from the hot tub, I looked down at the incoming note.

I can meet. The message was from "Damien Fraser, Fraser Farm." 6:00 p.m.

Okay. Guess that meant I had a plan for tomorrow. I'd worked hard to make it as an actress in L.A., but after five years, I was more than ready to move on. I'd never been cut out for Hollywood, but it had seemed like the thing to do when I'd been eighteen and desperate to escape the crap-storm of my life back on a small farm in Nebraska. I'd ended up enjoying my waitress job at a tearoom far more than acting, and became fast friends with the owner, Joelle. I'd learned how to cook, and to indulge my love of food in a way that didn't involve scarfing down pastries. At least not too often.

I definitely would have kept on at the tearoom for a few more years if it hadn't been for the complications and notoriety that *Gutsy Girl* brought with it. Reporters dug into my past and found out details that I was uncomfortable with. My sister's ex-husband—who'd always liked me a little too much—had made a few calls that had me itching to disappear again. I could not afford to have Rick show up on my doorstep and start messing with my head. Now that my sister had given him the boot, he seemed even more unstable. Scarier. Besides, I'd fought too hard to pull myself together after the ways he'd torn apart my self-confidence. And my family.

Now I just really needed to get out of L.A. and write my book. If I could pen the kind of relationship I wanted to have in real life, maybe I could finally excise the past. The hero in my story was going to be a turning point for me. If I could dream a new, healthy relationship, I could eventually make it happen, right?

So I saved my manuscript and shut down my computer, wishing I'd come up with a name for the guy on snowshoes in my story. He felt so alive, so familiar. Like a safe haven from all my real-world craziness.

As I set my laptop on the floor next to my sleeping bag in the echoing apartment, I tried not to think how lonely I must be to have fallen for a character in my own book.

# *1*

THEY SAY LIFE imitates art.

Which wouldn't have been so bad if I'd met a hot guy like Shaelynn did in my story. But no. *My* life imitated art because on my way to Sonoma the next day, my car broke down.

Worse, the lock on my SUV was busted because I hadn't taken the car in to the dealership to get it fixed after some creeps had vandalized it last week. So all that I owned sat on the shoulder of Highway 1, just south of Bodega, California. Any thief who came by would have the easiest job ever—if he happened to be interested in my prized collection of bonsai plants or size-eight flip-flops in every color known to man.

Yet as I walked up the road, the winter sun shining on my shoulders to tinge my fish-belly skin a lively pink, I knew the potential loss back at my used vehicle was not the worst of this day. My cell phone battery had died, so I couldn't call for help. Or make sure Damien Fraser had gotten the text I sent just before my phone died, saying I'd be late for our appointment. Now, I would miss the meeting with the owner of a property I'd been dying to purchase. It was a little plot of land with a perfect-sized building, on which I'd pinned all my hopes for the future.

I'd driven six and a half hours with my entire life packed into the back of that SUV in the hope I'd relocate up here. That I'd be able to move right into the charming little structure that had once served as a farm stand, close to a main road. I would rent it from the owner before the closing, and start fixing it up to be the tearoom of my dreams. Unrealistic? Maybe. But in his Craigslist ad, Damien Fraser had sounded very interested in unloading it ASAP.

Plus, I had a respectable down payment. I carried a cashier's check for 10K in my backpack, thanks to my *Gutsy Girl* winnings. Thieves would have done better to rob *me* as opposed to my SUV. I'd been careful not to touch a cent of the money after winning, knowing it was my ticket out of Los Angeles and out of the spotlight.

But now, thanks to my phone crapping out, the owner of my future tearoom might never know I was running late for our appointment. What if he ended up giving control of the sale to some hardball Realtor when I didn't show up, and I'd end up paying more and waiting longer for the deal to go through?

Damn it. *Damn it.*

I might have slid my backpack off and sat on the side of the road to sob at my misfortune if I hadn't held out a smidge of hope that maybe the building I was searching for was just around the next corner amid the olive groves crowding the northbound lane. I'd been telling myself that for two hours as I trudged up the road, because I was just enough of a glass-half-full girl that I maintained a shred of optimism. I had to be close.

When a truck pulled off the highway on the opposite side, I didn't think anything of it at first. I assumed the driver probably needed to make a phone call or send a text or something. Still, thinking about that cashier's check in my bag, I monitored the situation. I hadn't survived in Hollywood that first year I moved to the West Coast from Nebraska by being oblivious.

So when the door of the oversize pickup opened with a squeak, I looked.

And saw the hottest guy ever.

Now, maybe it was the heat that seemed to spotlight this hunky slab of muscle and manhood as he stood beside the open door of the truck. He glistened with sweat despite a temperature that probably reached only the mid-sixties. He took the tail of a well-worn T-shirt and used it to mop his forehead.

In that moment, his abs were exposed to my dazed, spellbound eyes. He was pinup sexy. Lean and taut, he looked like he'd pulled about two million inverted push-ups to achieve so much delicious definition in that six-pack. Better yet, he was tanned bronze and I felt like I'd been given a VIP pass to the hottest show on earth.

What a gift in an otherwise hellacious day. My heroine Shaelynn couldn't have done any better.

"Are you Miranda Cortland?"

I shook my head to clear it of fantasies that grew

more explicit by the minute. The demigod across the road did *not* just talk to me.

I realized I'd stopped to stare, and felt just the slightest twinge of embarrassment to be caught in the act.

Giving him a lopsided smile, I told myself to keep moving. Then realized he'd somehow known my name.

"Excuse me?" I had to shout, since two cars barreled by in either direction.

"Are you Miranda?" he asked, his deep voice carrying easily over the distance. He slammed his door shut and jogged closer.

To me.

I blinked. Confused. Dry-mouthed.

Because now that I saw the guy's face, he was a whole lot more than just hot abs. Streaked with sweat and a light coating of dust, he looked like a local laborer in his T-shirt and jeans. Although, knowing good clothes when I saw them, from years of shopping vintage, I realized he wore very *good* clothes. Those boots and jeans were both out of my price range.

"Lady, are you okay?" He was now just a few feet away.

Hazel eyes narrowed in concern, he stood a good six inches taller than me. His dark hair was close cropped and matched the dark stubble sprinkled along his jaw. Wicked cheekbones made him look a bit Native American. A prominent blade of a nose and full lips only added to his appeal.

I remembered the words I'd written to describe the hero of my book. *An arresting face. Strong. Handsome.*

"I'm *fine*," I said, with a bit too much enthusiasm.

What I meant to say, actually, was "*You're* fine." But he stared at me like I might have mental health issues, so I struggled to pull myself out of the sexy-man–induced delirium. He looked like the hero I'd dreamed up before I even laid eyes on this guy. "That is, I broke down a few miles back, but I don't think I'm far from my destination."

Belatedly, I realized I should have asked to borrow his cell phone. Or truck. Or his body.

"Right. Miranda Cortland?"

Holy crap. He really *did* know me. For a moment, I worried that he'd recognized me from *Gutsy Girl*. But he didn't fit the show's demographic. And now that I started to get a grip on the situation, I comprehended that he appeared very irritated. Highly annoyed.

Downright surly, even.

"Oh, God." I put the pieces together and felt like an idiot. "Are you Damien Fraser? Did that last text message I sent actually go through?"

The screen had faded to black a second after I'd hit Send on my SOS message to him.

"I didn't get it until a few minutes ago. I was working in one of the pastures." He didn't confirm his identity, but I guess he didn't need to. His gaze roamed over me, assessing. As if I was the one who was sweaty and dirty from a day in the fields. Somehow, I'd assumed "Fraser Farm" was meant more as a picturesque description than an actual farm…with animals.

But Damien Fraser of Fraser Farm was technically listed as the seller of the property that I wanted so badly. I stood straighter, wishing we'd met when I looked more like a serious real estate buyer and less like a college student on spring break. Or a fugitive from Tinsel Town. I'd stripped off my neon-green lace shirt an hour ago to wrap around my head, turban-style. I'd warmed up in a hurry once I started my long walk with a heavy pack on my shoulders. Plus, wrapping the shirt around my hair helped prevent me from being recognized after my recent notoriety. But it left me wearing a pink floral tee that occasionally exposed my belly-button ring. A snake with a sapphire eye. It had been my gift to myself for meeting my weight loss goals a few months after moving to L.A. and away from my dysfunctional family.

"I'm just so glad it reached you," I blurted, yanking the lace off my head, a trick that probably left my thick, ash-blond curls standing on end. "I mean, I've had a few hours to obsess over what might happen when I didn't show up for our appointment. Like, that you'd sell to someone else. Or refuse to sell to me on principle, because I wasted your time...."

Midsentence, it occurred to me that I'd broken every rule for savvy real estate shopping. I'd let the seller know how much I wanted what he had.

"Would you like to see the property now?" He hadn't interrupted me or anything, but I sensed he didn't want to waste time chatting about my "might have" scenarios.

Which I respected. But between my outfit and my chattering, I just knew he thought I was some flighty Hollywood chick with more hair than brains.

"Sure. But can I ride with you?" I had checked him out online and he had big-time ties to the community as a Thoroughbred breeder developing an upscale business selling mega-expensive racehorses.

He didn't strike me as the serial-killer type, even if he was a bit dirtier than I'd expected. Was I too swayed by his broad shoulders? Or by the fact that he was just what I'd pictured when I dreamed up the guy in my secret novel?

Now I'd never be able to see any other face but his when Shaelynn got back to her hot tub adventures. Lucky girl.

"Where'd you break down?" Frowning, he squinted against the glare from the late afternoon sun as he peered down the road behind me. "Is your car out of the way of traffic?"

"It's on the shoulder," I assured him, feeling an unreasonable need to have him view me as a responsible citizen. "It should be fine except…"

"What?" Hazel eyes searched mine, while a passerby shouted something incomprehensible at us out the window of a bright yellow sports car.

"Er…" I noticed the canary-colored vehicle threw on its brakes. Now I *really* wished I'd kept the turban on my head. "The lock is broken on my SUV—"

"C'mon." Damien Fraser gestured for me to follow him toward the road and his massive pickup truck. "I've got some chains in the back."

Okay. I won't say where my mind went on learning *that* particular bit of trivia. Maybe I'd been spending too much time daydreaming up plot points for my secret novel. I focused on darting across Highway 1 without getting killed, all the while keeping a weather eye on the situation with the vintage yellow Porsche, which had pulled over fifty yards ahead.

"Miranda Cortland?" a woman shouted out the window of the Porsche, alerting me to potential trouble.

I scrambled into the passenger seat of the Ford 450—a fact I knew only because it said so in chrome along one side.

"Friend of yours?" Damien asked as he climbed into the driver's seat, his size, warmth and general masculinity filling the cab. He kept his eye out the window on the sports car.

"No." I didn't need to look. I had become a recognizable face after the ten-week reality show I'd been on had turned into a surprise hit. I'd fallen into the job after a nice casting director who'd turned me down for virtually everything I'd ever tested for with her had recommended me.

While the show featured a few C-list celebrities competing in acts of daring to see who was the "Gutsiest Girl," there were also a few "real people" to fill out the cast. I'd been one of them, and the directors had focused on my waitressing job in an upscale tearoom. I'd been the Nice Girl competitor. The contestant no one expected to win. But when the other women had started plotting against each other, everyone forgot about me because…honestly, I'm not that memorable and I'm just too nice. So the last one standing had been yours truly.

"She sure can't drive worth a damn," Damien Fraser observed as he pulled into traffic and stomped on the accelerator, his triceps flexing as he cranked the wheel.

I gripped the armrest as the powerful engine all but

threw me backward into the seat. We put distance between us and the sports car in no time, and I decided
I liked Mr. Surly. He was a no-nonsense kind of guy,
different from the men I'd run across in Hollywood.
I pictured him revving the engine of his badass truck
to send members of the paparazzi scattering like ants
under a boot.

"Thanks for doing this." I knew I'd start chattering
soon if he didn't say something to fill the silence. Was
he wondering how the woman in the Porsche had known
me? Was he thinking I was a moron for not getting my
SUV tuned up before a big trip? Joelle had told me to,
but I hadn't wanted to spend any of the money I might
need for start-up cash. "I guess I left in such a hurry
this morning I didn't prepare as well as I should have."

I yanked the green lace top over the pink one, covering up the belly-button ring and making me look a
tad less disheveled.

"That you?" He pointed out my vehicle sitting at an
angle on the shoulder, so that it looked as if it had already given up the ghost.

"Yes. Whoa!" I slid sideways into the passenger door
as he flipped a U-turn and parked the truck in front of
my broken-down SUV.

He shoved open his own door without another word.

"Wait." I hurried to unbuckle and follow him. "I
can help."

I hated being Ms. Needy Female, but he was already
hooking a metal cable around my front bumper.

"I thought you were using chains?" Stepping carefully around some brush off the side of the highway, I watched him work.

"The winch kit will work best for starters." He pressed a lever to tighten the cable between my car and his. "Then we'll add a couple of chains for good measure. You want to put it in Neutral and flip on the hazards?"

"Uh, sure." I hoped this was safe. And while I was grateful to get my vehicle off the side of the road, I just hoped he wouldn't hold it against me that I'd really inconvenienced him.

More than anything, I wanted to get settled in my new digs, since I was technically homeless.

And yes, I knew most people would call it insanity to leave one apartment without securing another, but I had never been one to play it safe. For me, there was never a plan B. When trouble came my way, I dodged it and moved forward. Some might call it conflict avoidance. Whatever. I considered it taking charge of my life. In my own way, I overcame obstacles and moved on.

I put the old Highlander in Neutral as he'd asked, and switched on the hazards, then hurried back to his truck, since Damien was already climbing into the driver's seat. I got the impression he'd never wasted a second of time in his life.

Everything about Damien Fraser screamed that he did not suffer fools lightly. And me? I'd practically been born with a touch of foolishness. I considered it part of my charm. Up until recently, that is, when I realized that being on a reality show—if only for a few weeks—

had made it easier for people from my past to find me and harass me.

Too bad Rick, the main offender, hadn't stayed married to my sister. I'd always hoped him being married to Nina would keep the creep at arm's length, but since their divorce, he seemed way too eager to see me again.

As if.

"Ready?" I smiled up at my rescuer as I buckled my seat belt again, but the effort was wasted, since he shifted into low gear and focused on pulling out onto the highway.

More silence.

"So, Mr. Fraser—"

"Damien," he corrected, checking his side mirror.

"So, Damien. You have a Thoroughbred farm?" If I kept him talking, that meant I *wouldn't* be talking. Which meant I couldn't possibly say anything to potentially wreck my chances of buying the property.

"We breed racing stock. Sell shares in prospective winners."

I waited for him to elaborate, but this seemed to say it all as far as he was concerned. I knew something about farming from growing up in Nebraska, but a Thoroughbred operation was a far cry from a small family farm that specialized in a few hybrid kinds of corn.

"And the property you're selling. You just don't need it?" I took in the stark interior of the truck cab. There was no iPod plugged in or coffee mug in the cup holder. No mail on the seat.

Tough to be nosy when there were no good clues to work with.

"It's a good retail location with proximity to Highway 1, and there's already a building there. That little patch of property is worth more to me if I sell it rather than convert it into anything usable for the farm."

"Do you get many tourists up here?" I hadn't done much market research to see who might support a tearoom in this area. I figured I had Joelle in my corner to help me figure out how to make the business a success. Plus I'd had years to gather ideas of my own while watching her work.

"We're situated right along the Coast Highway. Some people come out to California just to see the sights up and down this road."

And yet it looked plenty rural to my eyes. I'd been really enjoying the scenery until the SUV bit the dust a few miles back. There were trees and hills, the scent of the sea in the air. Every now and then you turned a corner and caught a view of the Pacific, so blue it made your eyes hurt.

This was going to be a big improvement over L.A. When I first moved there, I'd just wanted out of Nebraska and away from Rick's betrayal. He'd upgraded to my sister after leading me on, wooing me out of my virginity and making me feel like a total loser in bed. The guy was a head case, and he'd done more than a little damage to my mental well-being in the process.

My sister's response to the news that her future husband had already been a jerk to me and showed flashes of a scary-as-hell temper? "Stay away from my man." Not in so many words, but...yeah. Nina felt totally threatened and had been convinced *I'd* done the leading on.

So Los Angeles or New York had seemed like logical choices as big cities to get lost in and forget about my family. I had literally flipped a coin. No one seemed terribly disappointed when I didn't go back for Nina's wedding.

Now I knew myself better. I'd really enjoyed working at the Melrose Tearoom in L.A. but thought a business like that in a quieter area would be more fulfilling. Less of a spotlight. More anonymity after the dumb reputation I'd gained from *Gutsy Girl*. Plus, I guess I hadn't lost my love of wide-open spaces. A part of me would always miss Nebraska.

But I'd learned to love the Pacific and the sense of peace the West Coast gave me. The Sonoma area had looked perfect when I'd been hunting online for likely places to open a shop.

Damien switched on his blinker and turned off to the right, near a small sign for Fraser Farm.

Intrigued, I saw four rail fences on either side and wondered if I'd missed the property I wanted to buy. It felt as if we'd turned right into horse country, with Thoroughbreds swishing their tails in green fields dotted with shade trees.

"Here it is." He pulled off the road to the left, in front of the building I'd seen online. It looked smaller in reality, probably because it was surrounded by vast expanses of horse pasture.

That didn't deter me. I slipped out of the passenger

seat and hopped down to the ground, feeling the pull of destiny.

The structure resembled a bungalow, with a wide porch, where I could imagine setting up a few outdoor tables. There was enough space for a small parking lot; no doubt it had served as one in the building's former life as a farm stand. I might be able to squeeze in a little garden around a patio if I used the space wisely.

I was already through the door, dreaming about how to convert the walls into shelves full of teas and tea-related products to sell to happy wine-country tourists, when I heard Damien clear his throat behind me. I turned, unsure how long I'd been planning my future in a total mental fog.

"Does it suit your purposes, Ms. Cortland?" His close proximity was not an unpleasant feeling. If I shut my eyes, I could imagine myself backing against him. Leaning into all that maleness.

What was it about him that had me thinking sexy thoughts so easily?

"Miranda. And yes. Very nicely." There was a studio upstairs that would be quite enough room for living space. No one from my past would bother me—no one would even *find* me in the middle of a Sonoma County Thoroughbred farm.

I'd sell tea, bake scones and after hours I'd write my novel, under a pseudonym. In fact, I felt all the more compelled to write my book now that the hum of sexual attraction pulsed just below the surface of my skin. If ever I needed inspiration, I'd just look out my window and wait for Damien Fraser to ride by on a horse or in a pickup.

Definitely liking this vision of my future.

"You said in your original email that you hoped to put a tearoom here?" he prodded.

"Yes." I tried to think about business details and not secret fantasies, but I was really distracted, imagining what he'd look like astride a horse.

Mmm.

"If I sell it to you, I'd need you to commit to that. The contract would include a stipulation that I'd have some say in the kind of business operating here. We can work that out with the lawyers, but I want to be up front with you."

I had no idea about the legality of that, but I understood why he'd want that kind of control, since my little piece of property would essentially be surrounded by his.

"Certainly." I set my backpack on the scarred hardwood floor that would gleam after I refinished it. I dug through my things to find my wallet, so I could hand the man my check and unpack a few things before it got dark.

I noticed the electricity had been turned off, so I wanted to get started ASAP, while I could still see.

From outside, a man's voice called. "Mr. Fraser?"

"In here, Scotty." Damien backed up a step and opened the creaking front door, allowing a wide swath of sunlight into the main floor.

A wiry young guy stepped inside. He wore a trucker's cap, with a big pair of old-fashioned headphones clamped around his ears. I could hear the wailing steel guitar and fiddle music from where I stood across the room, so I had no idea how he heard anything else.

I smiled at him, ready to make his acquaintance. But when his eyes met mine, I knew.

I'd been recognized.

My heart sank even as his face lit up.

"Miranda Cortland?" He shoved off his headphones and stepped closer, with the familiarity of someone who'd known me all his life. "No freaking way. The Nebraska Backstabber in my own backyard."

I swallowed hard, hating that stupid nickname the press had jumped on. Resenting that they'd dug up details about my past, even though I'd listed "Los Angeles" as my hometown.

"Scotty." Damien did not sound amused. His hazel eyes flashed a deeper brown and he tugged the kid back a step. "What the hell kind of manners are those?"

I would have been touched by that moment of chivalry if I wasn't sure that Damien Fraser would turn on me in another minute.

"It's okay," I rushed to explain. "Just a dumb nickname the media stuck me with after I won a reality TV show." If I downplayed it, maybe he'd let it drop.

Of course, Joelle had tried ignoring it when I returned to work at her tearoom in L.A. At first, she hoped my notoriety would be good for business. But two weeks in, she was so fed up with the paparazzi harassing the other employees for an "angle" about me, and Hollywood watchers clogging up the tearoom so her real customers couldn't get a seat, she'd asked me to take a paid leave.

Seriously? I wasn't about to collect a check I didn't earn.

"Don't let her fool you, Mr. Fraser. She's totally famous." Scotty shut down his music and reached for his iPod. "See? The Nebraska Backstabber won last season's *Gutsy Girl* by stepping back and letting everyone else fight it out. It was totally epic."

He tried shoving the screen under his boss's nose, but Damien's eyes stayed locked on mine. "Maybe later. For now, can you finish up the fence on the northern pasture? I didn't get to the last couple of acres in the southwest corner by the creek."

"Yeah, boss, I'm on it. Wait until I tell my girlfriend about this." He was already texting as he walked out the door.

Belatedly, I remembered that cashier's check in my hand. More than happy to change the topic, I offered the down payment to Damien.

"I'm sure any way you write the contract will be fine," I reminded him, all the while crossing my fingers.

*Take the check. Take the check.*

He didn't take the check. His square jaw flexed, a five o'clock shadow only making him more handsome. Too bad I knew what that uncompromising look meant.

"Miranda, this is going to be a problem."

# 2

HOT WOMEN WERE usually trouble.

Hot *Hollywood* women? They ought to come with a skull and crossbones taped to their foreheads. The potential for danger was just too damn high.

Damien Fraser knew this firsthand, having been born the son of a prominent American director and a flamboyant Italian actress. Their affair had produced three sons neither had time for, and the boys had grown up without much supervision, which meant Damien had tangled with his fair share of grasping Hollywood actresses who'd wanted to date him because of his famous father. But since he'd moved to Sonoma County and taken up horse breeding—a calculated move to distance himself from the Fraser fame—he'd figured his days of dealing with this kind of crap were done.

"I don't understand." Miranda Cortland ran a weary hand through blond curl that went in every direction, her pale blue eyes shadowed with dark circles that didn't do a thing to diminish her appeal. "I love the place. I've got a deposit. You want to make a quick sale, here you go. I'd like to rent out the spot until the official closing, so I can throw in whatever you think is fair for a month's rent. Or two."

She dug deeper in her backpack and emerged with a wallet.

Damien scratched his forehead, which was smeared with dirt and sweat from his time in the fields. He couldn't make the pieces add up here. The woman was sunburned. Her car was old and in need of repair. Actually, all her stuff looked like it had seen better days; the hodgepodge collection of goods that he'd spotted inside the SUV appeared secondhand. She seemed down on her luck for a woman who'd just won a reality game show he'd never heard of—*Gutsy Girl.* That much definitely fit.

Miranda Cortland showed some serious bravado coming all the way up here to pitch him her idea, when she looked about as far from tearoom elegance as he could imagine. He was pretty sure she had permanent eyeliner tattooed around her lashes. Silver cuffs wrapped around her right earlobe the whole way down.

"The problem is this." He cracked open a window to let more air into the place and leaned back against a rough support beam. "I'm building a brand with Fraser Farm. And it's got to be upscale to support the growth I need in the Thoroughbred market."

He needed word of mouth among a small, elite client base.

"This tearoom will be elegant and charming. A perfect match." She crossed her arms at her midsection, right where he recalled seeing a silver belly-button ring in the shape of a snake.

Did she have any idea how much she stood out here? Not just in this part of the state, but on his farmland? In his mind? She was so bright and bold—from her yellow flip-flops with the big daisies between her toes to her lime-green lace camisole—it was like she operated on another frequency altogether.

"Unfortunately, the kind of crowd your high profile will draw may not reflect the brand I'm developing."

"That's incredibly elitist and also…incorrect." Her voice remained steady, but he sensed more than heard the strong emotions there.

Chances were good that Miranda Cortland was here only to get close to his famous family. He'd had that happen before. So if she sounded convincingly disappointed, she probably was. But mostly because she wouldn't be granted her "in" with a famous Hollywood producer-director. Hell, Damien's father, Thomas Fraser, ran an independent studio, so he was definitely the kind of connection someone like Miranda might seek out.

"Fair or not, I have to think about the growth of my small business, and I prefer to have some kind of store or restaurant on site that will cater to the clientele I want to attract." He'd posted as much in his Craigslist ad.

When you were starting a business, every dollar counted, so he really wanted to make this sale. Especially since he refused to take a cent from his obnoxiously wealthy family. He just wouldn't make the sale to Miranda Cortland.

"Heard and understood, as I explained in my email to you—"

"Yet you did not disclose your celebrity status, and I have personal reasons for not aligning myself with the film industry." He headed for the door, needing to get back to work. As much as he'd enjoyed the distraction of a female that wasn't equine, he had ten other places he needed to be. His payroll was already ridiculously high with the specialized talent this kind of operation required, so until he could afford more help, he often had to be everywhere at once. "You're welcome to leave your vehicle here for as long as necessary. Would you like a ride anywhere?"

"No." She shook her head and backed up a step, as if she was going to follow him outside. "Can I just—please. Let me just show you one thing before you leave."

She held up her faded floral backpack, making a barrier between him and the door. He wasn't sure if she meant to slow him down or if the thing she wanted him to see was inside the bag. He noticed there were pins all over it—a cat with a hair bow in pink crystals, a few metal buttons advertising hole-in-the-wall nightclubs, a miniature L.A. Raiders jersey. The bag looked as if it had been around the world and back.

"I can't stay much longer." He held up his phone, showing a video feed of a birthing stable. "I've got a mare going into labor."

"Fine." Miranda was already setting her pack on the floor again and digging inside the bottomless interior. The sight of her sunburned arms and the bump of each vertebra showing through her tank top felt like chastisements.

What if she really was in need of a break? Something about her bravado—in spite of whatever personal issues she was dealing with—spoke to him on a gut level. He'd gambled everything to escape Hollywood once, too.

"I need some air." Mostly because the woman smelled like peaches and he wanted to inhale her. He struggled not to feel sympathetic toward her. Or even more attracted. "So let's talk outside."

"Yes." She followed him out onto the narrow porch, where two faded rockers still sat from the building's long-ago use as a farm stand. "Just take a look at these before you give me your final answer."

She held two pieces of paper in her hand. Actually, one sheet and one large photograph.

"I drew this last night when I couldn't sleep." She flipped the paper and handed it to him. "I think the look is very much in keeping with what you'd want to enhance your Thoroughbred business...."

She kept talking, but he was too distracted by the pencil sketch to pay attention. She'd drawn the farm stand building from the outside, but there was new life in it. Flowers bloomed in boxes attached to the front windows by iron brackets. Pillows and blankets were thrown over more rocking chairs on the porch, while round tables underneath big umbrellas made up a second tier of outdoor seating on a flagstone patio. The sketch was so detailed he could see some kind of flowering moss between the flagstones. A banner blew in an imaginary breeze, the flag depicting a steaming cup of tea and the name Under the Oaks.

"...I couldn't draw the inside because you hadn't posted any pictures." Miranda was still speaking. "I'm not sure I'd really call it Under the Oaks, but it fits because of the trees and—"

"And it's a racing term. Yeah. I know." The whole thing was elegant and charming, just as she'd promised. He had to admit the picture she'd drawn was appealing and exactly the kind of operation he'd envisioned to complement his growing business. He actually had a few rooms to accommodate guests who visited their horses on site, but as of now, there were no facilities for feeding visitors.

The tearoom could fill the gap for some food service. Except that she could be full of B.S. about what she'd do with a tearoom. What were the chances a young actress who'd just experienced success on a reality show would really want to come live in the anonymity of Sonoma? No, damn it. She was only conning him, to get close to the Fraser fame.

"You could have input, of course, if my take on this is too cute. I could make it more horse-themed. Lots of hunter-green and burgundy, like a gentleman's den." She frowned at her sketch over his shoulder. "Usually tearooms appeal to women, so—"

"It's great." He realized how close she stood. Her scent hypnotized him even as her springy blond curls brushed his shoulder. "The concept is well-targeted." He returned the paper to her and took a step back. "But just because you've got the right idea doesn't promise a successful execution."

She flipped a large photograph under his nose.

"This is the Melrose Tearoom, where I worked until a couple of weeks ago." She pointed to the picture of her with two smiling young women, at a table full of fancy silver trays, tiny sandwiches, crystal champagne flutes and porcelain teacups. In the background, a sunny atrium with uniformed waiters and linen-covered tables showed more of the same. "If you'd like to speak to my former boss, Joelle, she'll tell you I was personally responsible for much of her return business. I'm good at being a hostess, and I helped her stock a lot of unique specialty items that really increased her retail sales."

"Why did you leave?" He rechecked his phone to make sure the mare in the birthing stall still looked good. Damn it, he needed to just tell Miranda no and get back to work.

Memories of finding her walking north on Highway 1 kept biting him right in the conscience. She had to have been out there a couple hours before he'd found her. He'd been so engrossed getting the fence restrung that he hadn't checked his messages. She must have been determined to meet with him to make that long trek in the afternoon sun. To risk sunburn on her fair skin, when beauty was such a highly sought after commodity in her world.

"Honestly, I left because…" She met his gaze and bit her lip. "I attracted too much attention from that stupid TV show, but the fascination with stuff like that has a short shelf life. And up here, there are bound to be less tourists purposely looking for a brush with anyone remotely famous."

He'd heard enough. He handed her back the picture.

"Listen, if this was just some random piece of property, I would sell it to you in a minute." He tucked his phone in the back pocket of his jeans. "But I've got too much at stake in a business where the overhead is staggering. I can't afford to have any operation on what is basically *my* property that might detract from what I'm trying to build."

He'd invested every cent of his finances and himself in the Thoroughbreds. This farm had given him stability and purpose at a time when he needed to escape escalating family drama. He'd built a very different kind of life here. A stable life. There were no more weekend trips to Europe to help his mother solve some so-called urgent crisis that turned out to be an uneven number of men versus women at her latest dinner party. No more scandals involving his father's revolving door of twenty-year-old girlfriends. Definitely no more would-be starlets who'd do "anything" for a chance to meet his father. Even pretend to give a rat's ass about Damien.

Now, he kept in touch with his brothers, Trey and Lucien. But he was finished with the movie business and he was done with his high-profile parents.

"Interest in the show is dying down," she pressed. "And I can make this tearoom kick butt."

He was already heading for his truck. "I'm sure you could, but I just can't take chances right now. If I get a bunch of tabloid reporters camping out on the property, it's going to scare off the clients I'll be inviting up here to check out the operation firsthand."

He'd worked too hard to take this place to the next level, and he owed it to the former owner, who was also his mentor—a man who'd been better to him than his own father. Ted Howard had provided a job that allowed Damien to feel productive when he'd parted ways with his family, at age seventeen. He'd also shown Damien a different lifestyle—one that valued hard work. Physical labor. Mental fortitude. It had been exactly what a screwed up Hollywood kid had needed to reroute his life. So Damien wasn't going to relax until Fraser Farm was an equestrian showplace and—more quietly, in a new part of the facility—a humane retirement home and retraining center for Thoroughbreds who didn't achieve racing stardom. That had been Ted Howard's dream, a dream the guy might not be around much longer to witness.

Damien's jaw flexed, his shoulders tensing at the thought. He wanted that dream, too. He'd bought into it at seventeen, while working part-time to earn enough to go to college, and he was fully committed now. This life had saved him, so he planned to make the most of it.

"I am not afraid of hard work." Miranda dogged his steps. "A tearoom has low overhead and I can get this place up and running before your next guests show up. I realize the car breaking down makes me look kind of, uh, low budget. But I've got enough investment capital stashed away for the tearoom. I just won't spend it on fluffy stuff. Like a car."

"Sorry." He paused before the driver's side door.

"But the offer stands if you need a ride. Actually, do you want me to take you somewhere now?" He'd been thinking one of his handymen could cart her around, but how rude would it be to just drive off and leave her stranded? Hell. He'd been an antisocial horse breeder for too damn long.

Checking out of the fast lane didn't mean he could quit society altogether.

"I've got nowhere to go." She stuffed her hands in the front pocket of her jeans, making him realize she was way too thin. Hot, yes. But she definitely looked in need of...

No. He would *not* think about her needs.

"You can't be serious. You've got a check for ten grand in that backpack, along with God knows what else." He had the feeling Miranda Cortland, *Gutsy Girl* winner and—according to Scotty—the famed Nebraska Backstabber, had a wide assortment of talents to fall back on.

He didn't think he wanted to be around when the backstabbing skill was revealed, although from what Scotty described, her method of winning the show hadn't sounded the least bit underhanded.

"My savings are all for a bankable business. And until I find another perfect opportunity—the way this one was *supposed* to be—I'm not spending a nickel unless I earn it. So...need any help here?" She peered around at the empty fenced pastures.

Damn. It. He could almost picture himself standing here as a seventeen-year-old kid, looking for a job and hoping against hope that Ted Howard would find a way to make him feel useful. Damien hardened his heart, knowing her motives couldn't be good.

"Not unless you know something about mares in labor," he drawled, even as he took out his phone to text Scotty, so the kid could drop her at the nearest hotel. Manners be damned, Damien couldn't deal with Miranda Cortland right now. He'd had a foaling attendant in the birthing stable all day, but he planned to take the night shift himself.

"Are you kidding? I grew up in the heart of Nebraska, surrounded by cornfields and cattle. I guarantee we think just as highly of our cows as you do your fancy racehorses." She tipped her chin at him, all bold defiance and attitude. "It just so happens I spent more time in the barns than I did in my own living room, thanks to a dysfunctional family."

Again, she reminded him of himself once upon a time. Hiding out from dysfunction? Yeah, he understood that. Still, he held firm. She had to go.

But when he checked his phone to send Scotty the SOS, he saw the video feed from the birthing stable, where Tallulah's Nine was circling with restless frustration.

Crap. The mare became front and center in his thoughts. That foal had been sired by one of his most promising studs, and he didn't have time to boot out Miranda.

"Then get in if you mean it. I've got a mare ready to foal tonight."

THREE HOURS LATER, I'd shoveled enough straw to fill that stable ten times over. Or so it seemed.

I stopped for a moment to wipe away the sweat on my forehead and check out the miracle going on at my feet, now covered by a pair of huge boots I'd borrowed from Fraser Farm's extremely well-equipped tack room.

Giving birth was a messy business, and since the foaling attendant—Bekkah, a local vet's assistant— was busy keeping both the mare and Damien calm, I took up the less glamorous job of keeping the birthing stall filled with fresh straw. Damien had told me twice I didn't need to, but since Scotty had a sick sister at home and couldn't stay to do the grunt work necessary to help Tallulah's Nine, I could tell Damien was glad I was there.

I knew how to stay out of the way. I'd done it from the time I was a pudgy-cheeked kid who didn't compare to my big sister's beauty. And I'll admit, getting into the horse breeder's good graces was definitely a high priority on my agenda now. My novel heroine, Shaelynn, wouldn't have just given up and gone home. Especially not once she ran across a hero as hot as Damien. Besides, I loved animals. And I hadn't had so much as a goldfish since leaving Nebraska. Yet another reason Fraser Farm would be ideal for me.

"Thanks, Miranda." Damien worked to clean the new bay foal, while Bekkah waited for the afterbirth, the sweet scent of new straw hanging in the air. "With any luck, we'll get this little guy nursing in the next hour, and then I can find someone else to sit with Tallulah. I just want to be sure there's no need to call in a vet for anything. After that I'll be able to take you home. Or wherever you're staying."

"Why don't I sit with her tonight?" I offered, stroking the mare's nose. "I'll be able to tell if she's comfortable." I peered around the exhausted horse's flanks to look at Bekkah for confirmation. "Right? Putting a new mother at ease shouldn't be hard."

My father's small farm hadn't been much, focused more on hybrid varieties of corn than the animals. But my dad had been old-school about farming, and just enough of a doomsday believer to think we ought to have access to our own milk and eggs. The cows and chickens had provided me with dang good company during the worst of my teen years.

"You guys will both have to fight me for the right to stay by her," the foaling attendant retorted, a few long, dark strands of hair slipping out from under a worn Fraser Farm hat to hide one eye. "I've only been doing this for two years and every time it just…amazes me. I'm not going home anytime soon."

Even if I hadn't seen her face and the wonder in her deep brown eyes, I would have been able to hear it in her voice. I admired that kind of joy in a job. Moreover, I wished I could find it for myself. I don't know what had made me think I'd ever be fulfilled as an actress. Yikes. Never trust the decisions you make at eighteen. Especially when they are based on putting distance between yourself and a creepy man.

"You know there's a bed if you want to catch some rest," Damien reminded her, his voice warmer, kinder than it seemed toward me. Not that I was jealous or anything. But it made me curious.

"For sure." Bekkah nodded. "Looks like she's ready—"

The mare's contractions yielded the afterbirth that Bekkah had been waiting for. This part was a bigger deal with a Thoroughbred than a cow, I'd gathered. With a horse, it was important that none of the placenta was retained, so Bekkah would have to inspect the whole thing to be sure no pieces were missing that could cause infection in the mare.

Thankfully, the tack room had also been well stocked with gloves.

"Miranda," Damien said sharply, while I watched Bekkah work. Peering his way, I followed his gaze and saw the foal trying to stand.

Awkward legs and knobby knees struggled to coordinate their efforts. The bay colt wobbled. Leaving the shovel behind, I hurried to Damien's side. I didn't know if we were supposed to help the animal or not, but Damien seemed content just to watch. When the newborn got all the way to his feet, he took a step and tested those long, skinny limbs.

"Wow," I breathed softly, meeting Damien's hazel eyes over the little creature's scruffy head. "Incredible."

Damien didn't say anything. But his smile warmed me to my toes, our shared moment not needing any words. It felt special just to be there to see the foal standing on those precarious legs, instinctively seeking out its mama in the stall. And, okay, maybe I melted inside to see this big, badass dude—he had chains in his truck—so touched by the sight of the little animal.

I'm not sure how much more time passed before Bekkah declared the placenta intact, and Tallulah's Nine was cleared from having a vet visit until the morning. I mucked the stable once more so the new mom—a first-timer, apparently—and her foal were clean and comfy for the night. Bekkah and Damien agreed that she'd call right away if she had any concerns. I washed up and stepped outside the big, U-shaped barn and into the moonlight. There were at least thirty stalls in this facility, each with access to fresh air, while giving the animals plenty of shelter and protection, too. I heard more than saw the other horses nearby. When we'd rushed into the barn earlier, I hadn't noticed many other horses, but then, maybe they'd been in a pasture before sundown.

The soft creak of a door alerted me that Damien had joined me. Turning, I saw his broad shoulders emerge from the shadows of the building. His boots scuffed an even rhythm over the stonework surrounding the large fountain in the middle of the U.

"I'm tempted to wade right in there." I lifted my face to the mist, even though the temperature had dropped when the sun went down. I'd washed up at a utility sink inside the barn, but still, I needed a major dousing. "You've got a beautiful facility here."

"Thanks." He sank onto the ledge of the fountain, even though there were benches built around it at regular intervals. "When I bought the place three years ago, it was half the size it is now. At the time, I thought that add-ons like the fountain and the jogging paths around the property would be overkill, but after seeing some other Thoroughbred operations, I knew I had to up the ante if I wanted to compete."

"What made you want to be in the business?" I was curious about his background. Although he'd seemed a bit anxious during the foaling this evening, it wasn't the nervousness of a first-timer. He'd done that sort of thing before, I could tell.

His concern was either from a genuine love of animals or, perhaps, worry about his investment. Maybe both. I knew Thoroughbreds were mega-expensive. I couldn't begin to guess how much that mare or her new foal might be worth.

"I graduated high school early and moved up here to go to college away from family." He dipped a hand in the fountain and ran wet fingers along his forehead. "I worked here for the former owner while I put myself through Sonoma State."

I sat beside him, grateful to have a conversation that wasn't about the sale of his building, or my notoriety. I definitely liked him, and not just because he was mega-hot. Even if his vision for Fraser Farm was an obstacle to my tearoom, I couldn't help but admire his commitment. More than that, I still remembered the look on his face when he'd watched the foal stand for the first time.

"How long did you work here before you bought the place?" I put my feet on the ledge, tucking my knees under my chin while we talked. I was cooling down now that we were out of the stables, especially when the breeze occasionally blew the mist from the fountain onto my arms. It went right through my lace blouse.

"Off and on for six years. Even after I did a business internship overseas, the owner convinced me to come back here and apply some of what I'd learned to upgrade his operations." Damien folded his arms across his chest, staring off into the distance, where I could see lights from what was probably his house. "He also convinced me to buy my own racehorse."

"Really?" I sounded more surprised than I should have. "I mean, I guess it stands to reason that you must like racing. But I picture Thoroughbred racing as a very upscale sport, and today I've seen a very...er, earthy side of you."

He laughed and that deep, warm sound chased off some of the chill I'd been feeling.

"The behind-the-scenes route to the winner's circle isn't exactly littered with roses. But my friend had given me a hell of a deal on the horse he sold me—Learn From Your Mistakes—and I started winning races."

"Learn From Your Mistakes?" I had to smile. "Sounds like a horse I should have bought."

"He turned out lucky for me. I made enough off his racing winnings to invest in two more horses. They both paid off even better than my first." Damien's voice quieted. "Little did I know Ted was trying to help me earn enough money to make a down payment on this place and take it over."

"He sounds very generous." I thought about my own winnings from *Gutsy Girl*. I wanted so much to put that money to work for me the same way Damien had made his horse's earnings pay off with smart investments. "So then you bought him out?"

The sound of a soft, horsey snort came from one of the nearby stables, the scent of hay on the breeze.

"He was diagnosed with cancer and wanted to spend the rest of his time on a beach in Costa Rica, but he'd made commitments to other owners, since he boarded horses here. He was in a hurry to sell, but wanted to put the farm in the hands of someone who would honor those obligations and fulfill his other dream, of opening a Thoroughbred retirement and retraining facility."

"Retraining facility?"

"For horses that don't make the cut on the racing circuit. Too often, those Thoroughbreds who don't start winning early in their career aren't given a long enough chance to prove their worth. But there are a lot of options for them. Show horses. Pleasure horses. They just need a different kind of training. So we're doing that here."

"That's a great idea." I'd noticed construction equipment and new barns in the distance. I hadn't expected that development would be for such humane purposes.

"If I make enough profit on one side of the business, it just might support the other. But the farm turned out to be a second chance for me. I guess I liked the idea of giving the Thoroughbreds second chances, too." He shrugged. "Besides, I got the place for a bargain. But when I tried to give Ted more, he only ended up buying the architectural plans for the next phase of development he'd planned for the farm."

"So he put the money back into the business, anyhow."

"Yeah. He's doing well, too, healthwise. If I don't

keep him updated on the farm, he hounds me for information. I can tell he misses it."

"And all of a sudden you're a horse breeder." I tried to picture all that must have entailed, even as I wondered why Damien felt a debt to the former owner. I could tell he hadn't just bought the farm for a love of Thoroughbreds. He'd wanted to help out a friend. He'd wanted to give those hard-luck horses a second chance. That said something special about the kind of guy he was. "Although you must have been very familiar with the business if you worked here even as a teenager. You seemed comfortable enough in the birthing stall."

"I spent a small fortune having a vet by my side for the first few births after Ted left the farm, but I've learned what to look for now, so that if everything is going smoothly, I don't need that level of help."

"Bekkah's great," I observed, shivering involuntarily.

"Are you cold?"

"I'm fine." I hugged my knees tighter, unwilling to end this conversation and potentially have him drop me off at a local hotel. I couldn't think about my broken-down SUV and my broken-down life right now.

I needed a break from reporters looking to get a story on me, and digging into my past. Scotty hadn't told Damien that the Nebraska Backstabber nickname came more from me dating the man my sister later married—an incident that had been widely gossiped about in my small hometown before I left. Tabloid media had latched on to that nickname with both hands, spinning it into a bigger story after my unlikely win.

Little did they know that Rick had only used me to

get close to my family, close to my sister, who'd always been "the pretty one." His defection had hurt when he'd started dating Nina, but I'd gotten over it when I realized he was a bit of a sociopath—a charming liar whose brooding intensity covered a mass of insecurities more widespread than mine. Not that I could convince Nina of that at the time. She'd had to figure it out on her own. The fact that he was trying to connect with me so soon after his divorce did not bode well, but I could be anonymous here.

"Look, Miranda, I'm not going to kick you out if you need a place to stay." Getting to his feet, Damien offered me a hand. "You were great back there, helping out without being asked."

I stared at his hand for a moment. Touching him, even in such an innocuous way, seemed like something that would be…significant.

"I didn't mind." Carefully, I laid my fingers along his palm, waiting for the pleasure of it to subside into something more tame and appropriate, considering we'd only just met. "It reminded me of home. The nice parts of home, that is."

My voice hit a husky note that I hoped he would attribute to sentimentality instead of raw attraction. But I was drawn to Damien in a way I'd never been drawn to any other man.

For a woman like me, with the kind of dating history I'd had and the flat-out issues I had with sex and romance, this was a daunting realization. It felt encouraging in some ways, since it meant I still had a sensual fire inside me somewhere. Worrisome in other ways, since I couldn't imagine how I'd ever act on what I felt.

The attraction seemed exciting and scary at the same time.

"Well, I owe you." He gave my hand a gentle squeeze once I was on my feet, then let go of my fingers. "And I told you, I've got some extra rooms for guests who want to visit their horses on site. Why don't you stay in one of those tonight?"

I fisted my hand, holding the feel of him tight.

"As much as I hate to impose, that would really help me out." I wasn't going to dissemble and try to pretend I would be fine on my own.

Pride goes before a fall, right? Or something like that. I could not afford to be proud about this.

"Sure." He jerked a thumb in the direction of his pickup. "You need a ride back to your vehicle for a bag?"

"That'd be great." I followed him toward the truck, hope beating fresh in my heart, along with a girlie awareness of Damien that I could not allow to distract me.

I wanted to have a good working relationship with him for the sake of the tearoom I was determined to have. Plus, I liked the idea of being in his world so I could see what new ideas I might have for Shaelynn's hero. I might not be able to have him, but my fictional heroine could.

After all, it felt as if he'd walked out of my imagination and into my real life, waking a sleeping sensuality and stirring something…deeply appealing. If that wasn't a sign I was supposed to be here, I didn't know what was.

But I drew the line at acting on the heat I was feeling for Damien. Because there was no way I would let my issues with men interfere in what could still be the best business decision of my life.

# 3

EVEN BEFORE HE was fully conscious the next morning, Damien's gaze was drawn to the window of the building where he'd settled Miranda Cortland the night before. He'd put her in the best rooms he had, a large suite meant for a family or business partners who were travelling together.

The suite took up half the third floor over the offices. Many of the offices were still vacant while the business grew, but he had separate managers for the stallions, the broodmares and the yearlings, along with some administrative support people and a part-time transportation guy. Down the road, he'd need more exercisers, trainers and a sales director. Assuming he didn't bankrupt the whole outfit first.

Tearing his eyes away from the building where Miranda had slept, Damien hauled himself out of bed and vowed not to let her distract him from his work here. He had no intention of screwing up the operation that Ted Howard had entrusted him with. Damien had thrived under the man's guidance at a time when his every move had been chronicled in teen magazines. As the son of someone famous, he'd had cameras following him everywhere, even though he had no interest in the movie business. Damien's father had laughed off his worries, purposely shoving him into the spotlight to, as the old man put it, "get over himself." If not for Ted, Damien might have ended up completely severing ties with his father.

But he'd learned patience working here. Learned to separate himself from a father who thwarted his every effort to succeed, in some misguided attempt to make Damien "tougher." So he wasn't going to let his mentor down now, even though he was tempted to ignore what was best for the business and just sell that old farm stand to Miranda. After seeing her go to work in the foaling stall yesterday, he had to admire her grit.

A shower and a cup of coffee later, he headed out into the mist of another Northern California–winter morning, inhaling the earthy scents of the land that had saved his sorry ass when he'd first come here. The closest pastures were bordered by olive trees, the green-red of the fruit muted by a heavy coating of dew.

Carrying his second cup of coffee with him, he was making his way to the barn to check on Tallulah's Nine and the new foal when he heard a woman's off-key voice lifted in song.

"Bekkah?"

The singing stopped.

"Damien?" A dark head popped out of the birthing stall. And while the woman's features were familiar, they did not belong to the veterinarian's assistant. "Good morning."

"Miranda?" He blinked and refocused as he closed the distance between them, and realized she was alone with the foal and the mare. "Is it just me, or were you a blonde when you went to bed last night?"

Heat crawled up his spine as soon as he asked the question, the mention of Miranda and "bed" mingling the concepts damned attractively in his mind. He liked seeing her in a borrowed canvas coat with the Fraser Farm logo on it, as much as he'd liked seeing her in lace and a belly-button ring—both of which had figured heavily in his dreams the night before. To distract himself, he edged past her to stroke the mare's nose.

"Funny thing about that." She set aside a pitchfork that she must have been using to spread more straw. The stall appeared spotless, the scent of fresh hay stronger than the smell of horses. "I'd meant to dye my hair before I came up here, but it slipped my mind. After Scotty recognized me from *Gutsy Girl* yesterday, I remembered how much I needed to try life as a brunette." She settled on a worn wooden stool in one corner of the stall. "I took over for Bekkah a few minutes ago so she could grab some breakfast, by the way."

He'd almost managed to forget that Miranda was an actress, until she'd brought up that show again.

He nodded, knowing he ought to be grateful for the reminder to keep his hands off her. He wasn't. "Bekkah sent me a few updates last night. Sounds like the foal has been nursing regularly."

"He looks really healthy, doesn't he?" Miranda settled her palm on the foal's flank, both animals calm and accepting of her presence.

It was beneficial to accustom the horses to handlers early in life, one of many reasons Damien liked having an attendant around the new foals. Better to think about that instead of the subtle curve of Miranda's hip.

"Thanks for checking on them." He liked a woman who wasn't afraid to get her hands dirty. So different from every other Hollywood type he'd ever known.

He'd had a lot of experience with wannabe starlets, and most of them had been high maintenance. Cautious of their appearance at all times. His mom, in fact, had met his father back when she'd been acting. Motherhood had turned out to be a bit too hands-on for her.

"No problem." Miranda rubbed her fingers together, and when he saw a hint of her breath, Damien realized she must be cold.

"There are heavier jackets in the tack room, where you found the boots." He pointed to the big rubber footwear she'd helped herself to this morning. He'd insisted she wear them last night, since she couldn't go into the barns in flip-flops.

"Maybe in a minute." She gave him a sheepish grin. "I was actually trying to send a hint about the coffee."

She pointed toward his insulated mug.

He had the feeling she would have taken his and chugged straight from his cup.

"There's a fresh pot up at the house." Picturing her in his kitchen proved almost as potent as envisioning her in his bed. But when she didn't move to take him up on the offer, he extended his mug. "Or you can have—"

"Ohmigod. Thank you." She accepted the stainless-steel mug with both hands and drew it to her face so she could inhale the steam. "I've been awake most of the night, and when I smelled this, I was seized with this major caffeine craving."

Intrigued by her in spite of himself, Damien leaned against the stall wall while Tallulah's Nine nursed her foal. He noticed Miranda didn't wear nail polish, but her fingernails seemed to bear stickers of different flowers. A daisy on one thumb. A daffodil on the other. Some purple blooms on the pointer fingers. It was easy to see them, with her hands clutching the coffee cup. She treated drinking like a ritual, all her attention devoted to the task until she'd taken three long sips.

"Perfect." She caught his gaze with pale blue eyes shadowed by dark circles. "So what do you think of the color?"

"Hmm?" He'd been lost in thought about her eyes, so the question caught him off guard, as if she'd read his mind.

"Caramel taffy?" She held up a curl of her new dark hair. "I was picturing something more along the lines of butterscotch, but this is…brown."

"Sorrel." He found himself reaching for the lock of hair before he could stop himself. He lifted it to the light, examining it. "Chestnut."

Smoothing the strand between his fingers, he savored the silky softness. Underneath her big personality and crazy accessories, everything about her seemed delicate. Fragile, even. If he'd seen a photo of her as she looked right now, unmoving, he would imagine she had an elegant British accent and gentle demeanor. But her mobile features and expressive voice demanded as much attention as her bright clothes. While she was dressed more appropriately for the barn today, the thin, purple cotton T-shirt under her open jacket featured an image of a campy fortune-teller, and floral print jeans covered her long legs. She wore a green Fraser Farm hat over her newly colored hair, the short strands curling close to her jaw.

"Chestnut seems a far cry from caramel taffy, wouldn't you say?" She peered up at him and he remembered he still held one soft curl in his fingers.

He released it so fast it sprang back against her cheek with a bounce, making her blink.

"It looks…" Sexy. Hot. Tempting. "…nice." He cleared his throat and wished he could clear his thoughts, too. He needed a reset button on this morning, preferably going all the way back to the moment he'd woken up, so he could change that first thought about Miranda. "Did you want some breakfast?"

Maybe offering to feed her wasn't strictly in line with his desire to stop thinking about her. But damn it, she was too thin and too exhausted, with way too many shadows around her eyes. He didn't like the idea of sending her away without giving her a good meal or two. Hell, she'd worked so seamlessly at his side the day before that she'd earned that much, at least. He would have paid Scotty time and a half for working late with the foal.

"Depends." She winked at him over the rim of the

coffee cup, a gesture more friendly than flirtatious. "I have a hard time eating by myself. Can't sit still."

Did she have a tough time sleeping by herself, too? The question blared in his brain before he could filter it. She said she'd been awake half the night.

And with that visual jumping around in his head, he didn't dare offer her company for breakfast.

"I already ate." It was a lie, and it sounded like one, since he practically growled the words. But Miranda had been on his property for less than twenty-four hours and she'd already mounted a full-scale invasion of his thoughts. He needed to reinforce some personal defenses more than he needed those fences restrung in the north pasture.

"In that case...I'm good." She hopped to her feet, handing him back his coffee mug. "I have a lot of things I need to look into before I move on, anyhow. Would you mind if I stuck around a few more hours to use the wireless connection here? I've got to research some new places for a tearoom."

Guilt—both for denying her company at breakfast and for refusing to sell her the farm stand—weighed heavy on his shoulders.

"That's fine," he said slowly, distracted by the faint print of shiny lip gloss on the rim of his coffee mug. The urge to fit his mouth over that spot damn near overwhelmed him. "Stay as long as you need."

"Thank you." The warmth in her voice, the obvious gratitude, only made him feel like more of a heel. "And if it's all right with you, I might grab one of those heavier jackets, after all."

She stood close to him, gesturing past his shoulder in the direction of the tack room. For a moment, he breathed in her barely-there clean fragrance and the lemon scent of her shampoo, imagining touching her. Tasting her.

"Is that okay?" Her low voice twined around his senses, drawing him near. Her pale eyes turned a shade darker, her pulse fluttering fast in the smooth column of her throat.

His chest felt tight. Constricted. He wanted nothing more than to—

"Um, Damien?" She pointed past him. "May I…"

Belatedly, he realized he was blocking the door like a freaking oaf. Where the hell were his brains?

"Sorry." He stepped aside to let her pass, cursing himself, his thoughts and the unwanted attraction.

Yet as he watched her hurry by, her determined walk barely slowed by the heavy boots, Damien wondered if he'd imagined the shared moment, or if it had been there and Miranda Cortland was simply unwilling to acknowledge it.

"Um…Damien?" she called from somewhere else in the barn, her raised voice echoing around the high rafters.

He took a deep breath, inhaling hay and horses, reminding himself of his real life.

"Yeah?" He stepped into the wide aisle between the stalls.

Miranda stood near an open door at the far end of the barn, where sunlight poured in from outside.

"You've got some visitors asking for you out here."

She gestured toward the driveway looping around the fountain.

Frowning, he left the birthing stable and shot a quick text to Scotty to take over for him here. Damien squinted into the sunlight as he neared Miranda.

"Do you know who it is?" People didn't just drop by his farm. Especially not to see him. Maybe he just needed to redirect a prospective buyer to the yearlings manager, or put his stud director in touch with someone looking to breed a mare.

"Sounds like they want to look over your horses?" She tucked a dark curl behind one ear as he brushed past her, then tried to ignore the flare of heat she ignited.

"Damien!" a hearty male voice called as a young couple approached. "It's Charlie Whiteman. Thought we'd take you up on your offer to have a look around the place."

It took Damien a minute to place the guy—someone he'd met at his brother's bar a few weeks ago when he'd dropped by to help Lucien move equipment in the microbrewery. Luke had insisted he stay for a drink, which led to a conversation with Charlie Whiteman. Damien had told the guy he could drop by the farm anytime, because he was richer than Croesus and was looking to invest in some young bloodstock. But hadn't Damien also suggested "spring" might be the best time?

Damn.

The couple looked straight out of *Town and Country* in front of their sporty Mercedes, him in a khaki jacket and light blue dress shirt and his very blonde wife in a long plaid skirt with high leather riding boots. The guy had designed some kind of app and made huge amounts of money by the time he was twenty-five.

"I'm Miranda Cortland." Miranda spoke up to fill the awkward silence, holding out her hand to the wife.

"Violet Whiteman," the woman answered, extending her palm. "Charlie has been really looking forward to touring your property. He's mad for racehorses this month. I hope it's not a bad time for us to stay a few days?"

The guest suites weren't even finished. There was no food service in place unless Damien jumped in to personally cook for them. While he calculated the difficulty of finding last minute help to accommodate them, Miranda spread her arms wide and grinned.

"You'll love it here," she announced, twirling in place to showcase the three hundred sixty-degree view she'd laid eyes on only yesterday. But Damien had to hand it to her for making the unexpected pair feel welcome.

As she spun around, she caught his eye briefly, a questioning glance. He nodded, giving his approval for her efforts. And just like that, Miranda had made herself indispensable to him. Again.

She turned her megawatt smile back to Violet. "Did you want to see the barns, or would you rather come up to the house for a cup of tea?"

Violet couldn't say yes to tea fast enough. As she joined Miranda on a walk toward *his* house, Damien wondered how his temporarily homeless guest would find the kitchen, let alone the tea. But one thing was certain—Miranda wouldn't be leaving the farm today. And if she was already this comfortable in his kitchen, how much longer until he could make her even more at home in his bed?

*Shaelynn took his strong hand in her wet fingers, sinking deeper into the bubbles of the gigantic hot tub so she didn't inadvertently give him a free show. Because, of course, that would be brazen and inappropriate, right? Bad enough she'd made herself at home here while he was gone. But with her bare breasts close to the surface, her whole body responded to his touch and the wicked heat of his hazel gaze.*

"My name is Damien...."

I tapped out a revised scene for my heroine later that day as I relaxed in a den off the back of Damien's monstrous house. I'd spent all day either entertaining Violet Whiteman or prepping rooms for her and her husband in the half-finished wing that Damien had built for future guests. Since I'd taken the best suite for myself the night before, I'd had to move my stuff out and clean things up—change the linens, wash towels and whatnot.

I'd misplaced some stuff that I still needed to look for, but I was too tired tonight. The flash drive that had been in my laptop was missing, the biggest cause for concern, since I liked to back up my manuscript each time I worked on it. Knowing me, it had fallen out while I was moving things from the SUV into the guest room the night before. I'd been so tired after helping with the new foal, I'd hardly known my own name. I couldn't find a shirt I'd had from the *Gutsy Girl* show, either, but since my whole life had been stashed into a vehicle for the move, I guess the disorganization wasn't a big surprise.

Now I waited for Damien to get home so I could give him an update on his guests. Before Scotty left for the day, he'd told me his boss had escorted a stallion to another breeder about an hour away. I might have made myself comfortable in a different guest room if Damien had one, but the rest of the visitors' accommodations were unfinished, so I'd come here.

His house was huge. As was his hot tub, which I'd noticed while wandering around the massive house. Seeing it tucked in one corner of a lower-level living area had made me think of my manuscript, and I'd decided to write a little more. The words came faster, now that I could visualize the hero so well. I had come to think of Damien as the stranger who owned the house in the woods where my heroine had crashed her snowmobile. The man who sparked sexy thoughts in Shaelynn with a simple touch of his hand had become so real for me. So vivid and enticing…

*…She needed to release him before the moment turned awkward. But it was as if this gorgeous man had walked out of a sexy daydream when he'd appeared out of nowhere. The moment was surreal, as if the night had no consequences.*

*So, against all social conventions, she dragged his hand down into the water. Placing his palm on her bare left breast.*

*She watched his eyes widen for the briefest of moments before they narrowed. He plunged his hand deeper, cupping the weight of the taut mound and lifting it above the water. Her nipples pebbled to impossibly tight peaks as he lowered his head to capture one pink tip between his lips—*

"Miranda?"

The unmistakable male voice in the hall behind me made me sit up so fast I knocked over my laptop. It fell with a clunk to the thick carpet beneath the love seat.

"Here!" I announced myself, feeling oddly guilty and more than a little overheated. My heartbeat raced. "In the den."

I stood up and yanked the power cord stretched over my legs out of the device. I reclaimed the laptop from the floor and closed it with a click, ensuring the screen went dark.

"Hey," he offered by way of greeting, looking far too gorgeous in faded jeans and a long-sleeved black tee. "Sorry I left you here by yourself all day." He stepped deeper into the room and I noticed he'd taken off his shoes. There was something intimate about a man walking around in his socks. "I forgot about a stud appointment at a nearby farm. Normally I have a transportation guy come in to do that, but since it was close…"

With a weary sigh, he sank into the love seat I'd just vacated. He didn't finish his sentence, instead gesturing for me to sit beside him.

All I could see were his lips around my—that is, Shaelynn's—nipple. So awkward. So delicious. I had no experience handling situations like this. After Rick had mocked my virginal efforts in bed, making me feel graceless and undesirable, I'd really avoided intimacy. Really. As in, no sex since Rick.

I was so far out of my depth with Damien it was laughable. Still…a girl could dream.

"Can I get you some dinner?" he asked, thankfully unaware of me drooling over him as he scrubbed a hand through his thick, dark hair. "There's a Greek place up the road that caters."

He was so thoughtful. Was it any wonder I was lusting over a guy like him? If only I had a clue what to do with all that steam rushing through me.

"Actually…" I lowered myself back into the love seat, still clutching my computer to my chest. As if Damien might somehow see the screen, even though the laptop was turned off. Or as if he might notice those old love handles still spilling over the waistband of my jeans. "There are leftovers in your fridge if you want them. I saw a flyer for the Greek place in your phone book when I was trying to think about what to serve the Whitemans—"

"Crap. They needed dinner, didn't they?" He straightened, as if he was going to start prepping food right now.

At almost 9:00 p.m.

"I called Athena's and put a catered dinner for the Whitemans on your account. I hope that's okay, but Giorgos was totally cool and agreed with me that you'd probably want to feed your guests." I'd had fun chatting up the older guy who ran the restaurant, a man who seemed to know Damien well enough. And I still loved to *discuss* food even if I couldn't eat to my heart's content anymore. "He said he'd do smaller portions of several things so the Whitemans would definitely find something they liked. And since I was starving at the time, I had him send the stuff for gyros to your house, too."

"That's…" Damien glanced my way, his hazel eyes lingering "…really incredible of you."

Heat stirred inside me at that long look of his. Was it just because I was still seeing him through Shaelynn's eyes? Or was Damien Fraser seriously checking *me* out in real life? Whatever was happening between us was giving me major heart palpitations. I felt breathless. Confused.

That stuff simply did not happen to me. For years, I'd figured that incident with Rick had killed my libido for good. But I was honest-to-God turned on right now. Still, no matter how cool that was, I had to focus on my real reason for being here.

"If you sold the farm stand to me, I'd be around all the time," I reminded him. "I could help out with stuff like that. Send lunch and breakfast to your guests from the tearoom."

"And that's your motive for sticking around?" His eyebrows lowered over narrowed eyes. A blast of cold replaced the heat I'd been feeling a second ago.

"Well…kinda?" I shrugged. Did he think I'd just muck horse stalls and wash his guests' sheets out of the goodness of my heart? I mean, sure, I was a nice person and all, and I was crushing on the man big time. But I wouldn't have inserted myself into his life as his personal helper just for kicks. "That and the fact that I have no plan B for where to go next."

He frowned. "That's really why you helped out today? Hoping I'd sell you the farm stand?"

"Is that so hard to believe? Damien, that place is perfect for the business I want to build. And I really like it here." I'd been able to look out the floor-to-ceiling windows in the great room before the sun set, and take in the views of the olive trees. The horse pastures. It was very pastoral and peaceful, and I needed a lot more of that in my life. "It's beautiful."

"I thought maybe…" He reached toward my laptop and I shrank back. "Can I take that for you? You look ready to run any second."

"Oh." I loosened my hold. "I'll just…set it here." I put it on a big ottoman I'd used like a coffee table when I was writing.

And I made sure it stayed closed. Who knew what else Shaelynn and the newly named "D" had been up to since I'd left them?

My cheeks and neck warmed as I met Damien's gaze. "You were saying?"

Elbows on his knees, he threaded his fingers together.

"I was just going to say that I thought maybe the only reason you stuck around—the only reason you'd come here in the first place—was to get to my father the producer."

"Excuse me?" Had I checked out on part of this conversation while drooling over those massive hands of his? Even his forearms had muscle. I could see the shift of sinew where he'd shoved up his shirtsleeves.

"My dad is Thomas Fraser—"

"No way!" I blinked. Twice. Thomas Fraser was a huge force to be reckoned with in Hollywood. He was a legend for more than just movies. He'd acted in a few pictures once upon a time before going on to direct, produce and open a hugely successful independent film company. "You have to be kidding me."

"No. I wish I was."

"I would have never taken you for a Hollywood son." I couldn't begin to picture this serious, intense man in the superficial world that I'd operated in for the past six years. "What was that life even like?"

"I hated it," he answered flatly. "But no matter how much distance I put between myself and my family, I've still had plenty of film-industry followers approach me over the years, looking to get a script to my father, or trying to—"

"Oh, my God." I couldn't believe it. "You think I came here to, like…what? Audition for you? Get an acting recommendation? I was in one reality show and it was a disaster." I shot to my feet, offended that he thought I was that kind of person. "I'd have to be some kind of desperate to stalk you all the way to Sonoma County for the sake of a good word with your dad."

Damien rose, too. Stepped toward me.

"When I saw you pick up a pitchfork last night, I figured I'd been off base with that assumption." He gave me a halfhearted smile that let me see a dimple in his cheek.

My pulse raced like a teenager's. What was it about a damn dimple that could soothe a temper in a nanosecond?

"Last night was cool," I admitted. Seeing the little foal come into the world had been special. "I didn't even think about what I was doing. I just wanted to help."

I had never realized that I would miss being around barns and farms. I'd taken that world for granted when I lived at home, thinking it was as small-time and suffocating as my overly critical family. But maybe farm life had never been the problem at all. Being here had made me feel nostalgic for what I'd left behind. Of course, back then, I hadn't had a choice but to leave. I'd been reeling from my sister's betrayal hard on the heels of Rick's.

Having Nina ignore my warnings about the guy, having her think that I still wanted him had severed already shaky ties. I'd realized that if I was ever going to feel a sense of self-worth, I needed to start fresh.

"I figured as much," Damien was saying, and it took me a minute to remember what we'd been talking about. "And I really appreciated that. But then, when I walked in here tonight and it looked like you were trying to hide whatever you were working on at the computer—"

"What?" I felt dizzy. He knew about that?

Mortification chilled me as I remembered what I'd been writing.

Damien's mouth flattened into a thin line. "Is it a screenplay? A movie you want me to show my father?"

"No!" I denied it so strongly—so loudly—that *of*

*course* it sounded overly dramatic and false. "No. It's not a screenplay. It's just...private."

His gaze shot to the computer and I wanted to bury it. I should just confess the truth. But I was so flustered that anything I said might sound like a fib.

"It's embarrassing," I pleaded.

"Okay." He didn't sound convinced. "It's not my business, anyhow."

I could see my chances of ever purchasing the farm stand evaporating. Nerves twisted my gut. But I couldn't bring myself to tell him what I was really writing. Maybe if I was a well-adjusted, normal female, it wouldn't be a big deal to confess that I was writing a steamy, sexy novel. Or what *would* be a steamy, sexy novel, once I worked through a few mental reservations about the whole thing. I had issues with sex and romance. But this book was my ticket to dealing with all that.

"I've got to shower," he said suddenly, his voice cool. Distant. "There are guest rooms upstairs if you'd like to stay—"

"It's a naughty novel," I blurted.

For a long moment, he just stared back at me as if he'd misheard.

"What?"

"A, um, naughty book." I sounded like a middle school kid who got caught drawing naked pictures in her sketch pad. Not that I'd ever done such a thing. I cleared my throat. "I am writing an erotic novel," I clarified, probably sounding stuck-up and repressed. "It's definitely nothing I'd want your dad to make a movie about. So…good night."

Heart pounding wildly, I reached for my laptop and fled.

# 4

THE SHOWER THAT Damien took went from a way to get clean to a way to freeze out the red-hot images filling his brain with vivid clarity.

But when his fingers were wrinkled like prunes and he'd quit feeling his toes, he shut off the cold spray and admitted the sexual interest in Miranda Cortland wasn't going away any time soon. Toweling off, he debated how to approach her next, since he believed her 100 percent about not using him to get to his dad. Not even a world-class actress could fake the discomfort he'd seen in her when she'd confessed to…what she'd really been writing.

What surprised him was how secretive she'd been about the whole thing. In his mind, a woman who wrote explicit stories for fun would possess the kind of boldness that would protect her from being embarrassed about it, but obviously that was a faulty assumption.

After dressing, he cracked open the door of the master suite into the hall that led to the kitchen. He hadn't eaten and he was starving. The coast should be clear, since Miranda would most likely be locked up in whatever room she'd chosen for the night. He'd scared her off without fully meaning to. Yes, he'd wanted her to come clean if she was using him to get to his father. No, he hadn't meant to press her about something that was genuinely private and probably none of his business.

But damn.

Had she been writing an erotic romance in his den? Curled up in his chair while she dreamed of provocative encounters to describe in detail for her story? He needed that cold shower all over again and he'd been dressed for less than five minutes. The thought was making him crazy. And why did he feel as if someone was having sex in his house without inviting him? It made no sense and messed with his head.

Stalking through the quiet house, he guessed she must still be here, since he hadn't heard her leave. He'd polished off half the leftovers while standing at the kitchen counter when the front doorbell rang. Had something gone wrong in the barns?

Jogging toward the front of the house, he pulled the door open...only to find Violet Whiteman wearing a long gray sweater over what looked like expensive loungewear. Those were definitely slippers on her feet. Her eyes were bright. Wide.

"Is Miranda around?" She peered over his shoulder to take in the house behind him. She spoke fast. Breathlessly. "I know it's late and I'm so sorry to bother you, but I didn't realize who she was until just a minute ago, when I was online." She shook her head, blond hair swinging with the motion. "I've been trying all day to think why she looked familiar. I didn't recognize her as a brunette."

Tension tightened the back of Damien's neck. Just what he didn't want—Fraser Farm being overshadowed by a Hollywood connection. He needed to build their reputation on Thoroughbreds, not as some outpost for star-gazing.

"She's in bed," Damien explained, wondering why this woman felt the need to talk to Miranda so late. "But I can let her know you dropped by."

"Oh." Her face fell. She lowered her arms, which she'd been hugging against her. A small camera swung on a strap from one thin wrist. "I guess I will see her tomorrow. She'll still be here, won't she?" Violet's brow furrowed. "She lives here?"

Not exactly.

Although thinking about Miranda tucked in one of his beds, in a room inside *his* house, while she imagined erotic scenarios for her next book, made him feel ridiculously protective of her. And right now, he planned to respect her privacy.

"She'll be around tomorrow." He hoped.

In fact, just thinking about the possibility that she might take off without telling him—might have already done so—made him want to sprint up the stairs and see her with his own eyes.

He owed her an apology. Among other things. A better thank-you was definitely in order, as well. She'd worked too hard helping him out over the past two days for things between them to end on a sour note.

"Okay." Still, Violet Whiteman did not back off the threshold of his front door. She remained, indecisive. "I thought she was great on *Gutsy Girl*," she confided finally. "I know a lot of people said it was terrible how she gained everyone's friendship and then stepped aside while they all turned on each other, but that's simply ridiculous."

Violet rattled on as if he was totally clued in about the premise of the show. Normally, he would have found a way to politely edge her out the door. But he had to admit, he was more and more curious about the woman who'd dive-bombed into his life yesterday. Miranda was one hell of an interesting set of contradictions.

Runaway actress. Would-be tearoom proprietress. Capable stall mucker. Author of erotic fiction.

"So what did you think?" he asked Violet, since she was clearly dying to talk about the show.

"Are you kidding me?" She pumped her fist awkwardly, like a woman who'd never made the gesture. "Score one for the nice girls." She gave a little giggle and then covered it up behind one perfectly manicured hand—pale pink polish, white tips. Lowering her voice, she leaned closer to Damien. "Some of us who strive to play well with others—we get tired of people assuming that we're the doormats of the world. I thought it was great that Miranda used her natural sweetness to surprise everyone and win the game."

Behind him, inside the house, Damien heard a noise. A soft shuffle.

And suddenly, he was less interested in what Violet had to say and more interested in who might have overheard the conversation.

"I'll let Miranda know," he assured his visitor, stepping back and gripping the door. "Have a good night."

Smiling, Violet said all the things that a "nice" girl would in taking her leave. Damned if he didn't wonder what she *really* wanted to say to him, if indeed Miranda's character on *Gutsy Girl* was her secret role model. No doubt there was more to Violet Whiteman than met the eye.

As he closed the door, he stood still. Listening.

Soft footsteps retreated up the stairs to the second floor. Was it wrong of him to hurry so he could catch Miranda in the act?

"Nice girl?" he called as he moved toward the back of the house near the staircase. "She must not know about the eavesdropping habit."

He arrived at the base of the stairs in time to see her bare feet stop midway up. Miranda stood with her back to him, a blanket thrown around her shoulders like a shawl and a pair of silky turquoise pajama bottoms covering her legs.

She turned.

Her dark curls were clipped at the back of her head, her hair short enough that half of it sprang free to fall in her eyes. Beneath the blanket she wore a dark tank top, and he was pretty sure that was all. The waistband of her pajama pants was rolled down to just above her hips, a line of skin visible where her top ended and the bottoms started.

The snake's eye in her belly-button ring winked at him in the half-light of a hall sconce.

Miranda lifted her chin. "I wanted to make sure whoever was at the door wasn't here because of Stretch."

"Because of what?"

"Stretch. That's what I've been calling Tallulah's foal in my mind." She tugged the ends of the blue throw blanket tighter around her, covering up the bare skin at her midsection. "That little foal was the first thing I thought of when the doorbell rang."

"Me, too." And how strange that their lives and thoughts had synced so quickly. He would have never envisioned that kind of compatibility between him and any woman a few days ago, especially not a Hollywood runaway who'd blown into his life like a gale-force wind. "Violet was only here so she could see you. She had a camera."

"I'm not much for photo ops." Shaking her head with a rueful smile, Miranda sagged back against the banister and slid down to sit on a stair. "Especially not after the way that show treated me."

He moved toward her but didn't climb the steps. He dropped onto a tread below her. Still, the dim light and confines of the stairs—a wall on one side and the banister on the other—made for an intimate setting. Or maybe that was just because she was in his house, wrapped in his blanket, wearing pajamas.

That definitely could have been part of it.

"It's some kind of competition?" He'd never heard of *Gutsy Girl* until yesterday and hadn't found time to look it up online.

"There are a lot of team and individual challenges similar to what you might go through at boot camp. The show invited a bunch of diva-type women to go on it, minor celebs from other reality shows, along with a couple of 'regular women' like me to compete for the grand prize. Audiences had fun watching the high-maintenance women fall in the mud or burst into hysterics over climbing a rope."

"And you somehow won by making friends?" Damien peered up at her, surprised to discover her thigh was so close to his cheek.

Close enough that he could lean over and kiss her right there through the turquoise silk that featured—he now realized—a subtle print of trapeze-swinging monkeys. Okay, maybe it wasn't subtle. He just hadn't noticed it before.

She leaned forward on her elbows, stirring the air just enough that the scent of her soap or shampoo teased his nose and drew him nearer.

"You have to form alliances along the way and play that whole social mind game." Shrugging, she lost the blanket that had been around her shoulders. It slid down her back to rest on the step beside her. "But I'm not good at stuff like that, so I just concentrated on winning challenges and being myself. I guess some critics saw that as some kind of nefarious strategy. I think Hollywood is more comfortable with reality-game players who plot their approach openly and share their thoughts with viewers. I didn't share much of anything when the camera was on me, so now—because I won—I'm somehow seen as an evil schemer."

His eyes drank in the sight of her bare shoulders in the dark tank top, the graceful lines of her arms and neck an unexpected visual feast that had his mouth watering. He wanted to see more. To touch more. Taste any part of her he possibly could. With heat simmering in his veins, he lifted himself up to the step beside her and retrieved the fallen blue cashmere. Hardly thinking about what he was doing, he wrapped it around her again.

Their eyes met while he tucked the throw back where it belonged.

Making him realize what he was doing. The familiarity of the act.

He let go of the blanket. Drew back to his side of the stairway, even though that put only a couple more inches between them. His pulse throbbed, his body all too aware of hers now. What the hell was he thinking?

"Sounds like you were penalized for succeeding." He closed his eyes for a second and still saw her pale blue gaze in his memory. Her full, soft mouth.

And all he could think about was her penning a steamy book. Did she consider moments like this worthy of writing about, or was her novel full of more heated encounters? His body responded so strongly to that thought, he couldn't will away the reaction.

"The show's producers were looking for promotion angles the whole time. I happened to be a workable story for them as a so-called "backstabber," and they sold it with selective footage editing." She tipped her head against the spindles of the banister. "I don't necessarily have a problem with that, since I signed on for it, but I never imagined such a backlash over a television show."

He watched her toy with the fringe on the blanket that rested along one arm, and tried to rein himself in. He wanted to kiss her clothes off and explore what was underneath. To stretch her out right here and cover her. But he focused on her words instead, ignoring the heat coming off him in waves. She struck him as a woman who kept a tight rein on her passions.

"So you want to be more anonymous here." Sonoma wasn't some isolated hill country in the middle of nowhere, but then again, she wouldn't have the same notoriety as in L.A. "Just because of the show? Or because of the book, too?" His voice cracked. Not like a teen's. More like a parched man craving water. Or craving a woman. "Have you written others?"

"No," she said quickly, gesturing with the fringe. "This is a first."

He wanted to know more about the book, but she wasn't volunteering. Memories of her running out of the den, her laptop clutched to her chest, returned. This was a more reticent side of Miranda and he wasn't quite sure how to handle it. Did he make her nervous? He'd never been the world's most eloquent guy, but he definitely had never scared off a woman.

And no matter how much he was feeling the heat right now, he had the distinct impression that Miranda was feeling tense over on her side of the stairs. So he stuffed his attraction deeper and tried to keep her there, keep her talking, even though he'd rather be kissing her.

Thankfully, he still had enough presence of mind

to formulate a question and hold up his end of the conversation.

"Do you really think you could be happy running a tearoom in a place like this?"

WAS HE ACTUALLY considering selling to me?

I licked my lips and thought about the best way to answer. It would be unwise to jump on him and shout "Yes! Yes!" at the top of my lungs. But part of me wanted to. Especially because I sensed—hoped, really—that he was as turned on right now as I was. Or was that wishful thinking on my part?

Unfortunately, I could not be more clueless about guys. Nice guys, anyway. I knew plenty about losers.

Whatever Damien's mood, I was grateful for the question, since it kept us talking. I wasn't ready to go to bed when my thoughts were so full of this sexy, compelling man.

"I would love living up here," I assured him. "Hollywood was fun for a while—especially when I was eighteen and fresh from the Midwest. But I grew up in a rural setting and that feels more like home to me. Except…" How much to say about my past? "…I'm not close to my family or anything. So I don't have any desire to go back there."

That was true enough. My parents had a strong preference for my older sister. But the bigger issue had been Rick drooling on me and making free with my person even after he'd gotten engaged to Nina. Counseling a few years ago helped me see the way the guy had manipulated me, taking advantage of my youth and insecurities about my weight. I'd had a lot of guilt over what happened between us, which accounted for some of the messed up issues I had with guys now. Of course, knowing that rationally didn't just "fix" the problem. But my book—Shaelynn's story—was helping me with some of that.

I'd progressed to the point where I thought about sex more. And meeting Damien had definitely fast-forwarded the whole process.

"We have that in common. I'm definitely not close to my folks, either." Damien's jaw went tight. I could see that even though he was staring straight ahead.

Sitting midway up the staircase, we looked out over a big family room. Deep sectional seating surrounded a television at one end and a fireplace at the other. A fire blazed in a stone hearth and I wondered who'd started it, since Damien hadn't been around the house all day.

"You know, I remember reading your family's story in a magazine or somewhere." All three of Thomas Fraser's sons were reputed to be handsome, well-connected bachelors, even though their father's strong-arm tactics had driven two of them out of town. A third remained in the film business, but they'd had a strained relationship until recently. "Your oldest brother is making a movie with your dad soon, I think."

"So I've heard. I don't get back to Malibu very often." Damien's voice hit a gravelly note that probably revealed a little more emotion than he'd intended.

On instinct, I laid a hand on his shoulder, a normal, natural touch I'd shared with countless patrons at Jo-elle's tearoom. It offered comfort. Understanding.

But with Damien, my fingers buzzed as if I'd been shocked. Well, except that it felt *good*. Nerve endings awakened. My blood warmed. It felt like a magnet held my hand there, commanding my touch with an irresistible pull, making it impossible to draw back. I gazed down at my fingers, half expecting to see some kind of magical glow. It felt that freaking amazing. Inevitable.

Uncertain, I splayed my fingers wider to cover more terrain, since his sculpted muscle proved too broad to span with my hand. Warm and hard beneath the surface of his T-shirt, his body was uncompromisingly male.

He turned to face me, that strong sinew shifting under my touch. My heartbeat quickened at the look in his hazel eyes. I felt the connection between us as surely as if I'd penned the scene myself.

Only I would have written it for Shaelynn.

With *me* in the mix, I wasn't sure what would happen next. I usually retreated ten times before I let a guy kiss me, and by then the male in question normally lost interest. But right now, I didn't feel any need to run. I felt as if I'd lived through this moment in my book.

Except I had no idea how to move this scene forward. I wasn't scared or tense, the way men usually made me, but I had no idea what to say to make the kiss happen. A kiss I really, really wanted.

As if moved by my thoughts, Damien put one hand on the tread beside me and levered himself up a step. His big, strong body blocked out the glow of the fireplace, casting me in shadow until all I saw was him. My heart rate quickened. I swallowed hard.

"I want to kiss you." He announced it, which made

me melt inside a little, since I was more nervous than I'd realized.

I think I nodded. I tried to, anyway, but I was kind of hypnotized by the look in his eyes and the heat coming off him like a furnace. Vaguely, I wondered if I'd combust on contact. Or if a racing heart could send me into seizures.

"Do I make you nervous?" He brushed a gentle hand under my chin and along my jaw, his touch light and delicious.

Not wanting to address that particular question or even think about it, I blurted what I wanted.

"Please kiss me."

Then his lips were on mine and all that weird, anxious energy in me quieted. The gentle brush of his kiss was the sole focus of my attention. It was like his mouth spoke the language of my crazy, spun-up hormones and they all sighed with dreamy appreciation at his attention. And me? I couldn't believe my luck to have those warm hands on my waist, his fingers straying to the bare skin beneath the hem of my shirt. He steadied me as he kissed me, holding me still while his lips moved in a tantalizing dance over mine. Soft at first. And then, with a brief flick of his tongue along the seam of my lips, things turned sexy.

Hot.

Damien knew how to kiss. The hero of my book would, too, but I would have never known how to write about it without this thorough and unhurried demonstration. Damien savored me like fresh fruit at harvest time, tasting, nipping, licking. He made me feel delicious. My fingers sank deeper into his shoulders, clutching at the warm, soft cotton of his T-shirt and the strength beneath it. I liked feeling that strength, knowing all that power rippled in his body, yet he restrained it for my benefit. Somehow it made his gentleness even more of a gift.

Kissing his stubbled jaw, I breathed in the scent of his aftershave and hoped it lingered on my skin. He smelled fantastic.

I arched against him, seeking out more of his body, and that was another gift. He didn't rush me. He let me feel my way through the kiss, absorbing every detail at my own speed until I was comfortable. No, not comfortable. Hungry. It was *dis*comfort that drove me to rock my hips into his.

I needed him. Needed this.

The ragged growl didn't come from his mouth so much as it reverberated inside him. I felt it in my breasts, where my body touched his. Desire leaped to life inside me with new fierceness. I wrapped my arms all the way around his neck and deepened our kiss.

Damien responded in kind, his lips claiming mine fully. The hard length of his erection strained against my hip, the heat of him all but searing the fabric of my pajama pants.

He broke the kiss for a moment, gazing down at me in the dimness with hazel eyes lit by a fire within.

"Let me take you upstairs." He wrapped his hands around my back, making me realize that a stair tread had been digging into my spine, before he eased me away from it.

"No," I said quickly. Then, seeing the flicker of confusion in his gaze, I backpedaled. "It's not that I want to stop. I just…I'm afraid if we move, I'll…"

Freeze up? Have second thoughts?

I wasn't sure how to finish my sentence without revealing too much. Maybe I already had.

"Is everything okay?" He shifted away a fraction of an inch. Maybe he was only trying to give me room to breathe or room to think. But instead, I just felt the cold creeping in, and old insecurities rising up inside me.

*You'll never be half the woman your sister is....* The damning words from my past blared across my consciousness.

"Fine." It sounded like the lie that it was.

Damien's hands started to slide away, so I held them in place with mine. I wished I had the superpower to reverse time. I definitely wanted to rewind a few minutes.

"Wait." I tried to think how to explain myself. I didn't want to alienate him, and not just because I wanted to purchase the farm stand. I *liked* him. A lot.

I'd deal with what that meant later. Right now, I couldn't afford to ignore those sensual feelings he'd inspired in me that no one else could.

He stilled. Kept his hands where I wanted them. But there was a definite distance between us now. One that would remain unless I said something.

"The kiss was amazing." Just thinking about it stirred my insides and made me long to try it again. "And I would like more of them. More of—everything. I'm just going through some things that I'm still trying to sort out."

His shoulders straightened as he tensed.

"You care about…some other guy?"

"God, no." I shook my head. "Just the opposite. I'm still processing a lot of negative feelings for a mega-jerk in my past."

Some of the tension left him. Not all. He glanced down at where his hand rested just above my hip, and then he stroked that place softly with his fingers.

So. Nice.

"Is he the reason you left L.A.?"

A small, pleasurable shiver went through me at his touch.

"He's more the reason I left Nebraska." As soon as I said it, I realized that I sounded like a giant loser to still be wading through old baggage from six years ago. Obviously, I needed to try and explain myself. "He broke up with me to marry my sister, which was good and bad, since it kept him away from me, but also put another barrier between me and my family." Not that we'd ever gotten along all that well before. I'd been the afterthought daughter my whole life. "Then, five months ago, he finalized a divorce from Nina and now…I don't want to make it too easy for him to find me."

He'd left a voice mail message for me a few weeks ago saying he was planning a trip to the West Coast. That he'd see me soon. No way was I waiting for that to happen.

Damien's jaw worked as he frowned. "Did he hurt you?"

"Emotionally? Yes. Physically, no." I sighed, realizing I might as well just tell him. "He dated me when I was seventeen and going through a lot of stuff—on the rebound from being jilted at a homecoming dance, super insecure because I was the family black sheep and a bit overweight. Anyway, I really did like him for a while and he was the first guy I was ever with." I didn't add that Rick was also the *only* guy I'd ever been with. Instead, I met Damien's gaze and was grateful he hadn't moved away from me. "I thought I was in love."

"How old is this guy?" His fingers kept up their soft circling above my hip.

"Three years older than me." I tugged the cashmere throw higher on my shoulders. "The same age as Nina."

Damien nodded. "He broke up with you to marry your sister?"

"Pretty much." I didn't need to share all the sordid details to show what a bastard he'd been, lording it over me how much "better" my sister was when it came to pleasing a guy. It was easy to see how sick that was now. Back then, I'd kind of believed it. Nina was better than me at *everything.* Honor student, teacher's favorite, regional dressage champion… The list went on. "But then the rat bastard still tried to two-time us by coming on to me at family parties and basically manhandling me whenever he thought no one else could see."

"What'd your sister have to say about that?"

"She blamed me for trying to seduce him, and warned me I'd better stay away from her man. It was like a soap opera." Only much worse, because instead of watching the drama happen to your favorite characters on daytime TV from the comfort of a living room sofa, I had it happen to me in real life, and it had been 100 percent awful.

"Wow." Shaking his head, he brushed a light kiss on my shoulder through the blanket, and my heart squeezed tight with tenderness for him.

For years, I hadn't shared this story with anyone but a bargain-budget shrink, who'd helped me work through some of it. Now, it was nice to have Damien side with me.

"Yeah. Exactly." I debated what else to say, since I didn't want the night to turn into a pity-poor-me fest. I was putting that whole period behind me, methodically dealing with all the crap from my past. On the other hand, there was something else Damien needed to know about it. "Then, when I was on *Gutsy Girl,* one of the camera crews went to my hometown to talk to my family and interview people who knew me."

"Your family didn't spill that stuff on camera, I hope."

"No. But it wasn't difficult to find a friend of my sister's who called me a backstabber. In her words, I 'tried to break up Nina's marriage by flirting with her husband.'" I couldn't remember ever feeling so angry and betrayed as when I saw that footage. "But that's reality television, you know. Heavy on melodrama, light on reality."

"That's Hollywood—period." He shook his head. "Sorry you're dealing with the fallout from something that should have been over a long time ago."

"I should have known better when I agreed to do the show in the first place." I shrugged. "I guess I was romanced by the whole notion of being a gutsy girl."

Joelle had really encouraged me to do it, knowing

how hard I'd worked to become more fit ever since moving to Los Angeles. A lot of the challenges came easily to me because I was in such good shape. Winning *Gutsy Girl* had given me a new level of self-confidence. Now all that remained for me to really fix myself and heal the past? Ditch the sexual hang-ups. And the book was going to help me do that, I was certain.

"It takes guts to change your life. Sounds to me like you had plenty going for you before the show started."

"Yeah? Maybe you're right." I preferred to think of my life that way. Plus, I didn't want him feeling sorry for me. I wanted him to kiss me again someday. "But either way…that's the story behind why I'm writing my book."

My cheeks heated as I said it, but he deserved to know the truth.

"I don't get it." His dark brows came together in confusion. "What does the past have to do with writing an erotic novel?"

"I'm writing about what I *want* instead of…anything I've ever experienced."

His eyebrows shot up and his hand stilled on my hip.

He said nothing, but I noticed the way his breathing shifted. I felt the spike in temperature between us.

"That's one reason why the book is so important to me. It's helping me put the past to rest." I burned from attraction and self-consciousness at the same time, but I didn't let embarrassment hold me back from touching his chest. Feeling his heart beat beneath my palm.

I was the *Gutsy Girl* winner, damn it. I could do this. "I'm writing about what I want—sexually. And after we met, I realized that it was you."

# 5

DAMIEN CLENCHED HIS HANDS with the need to take Miranda upstairs. His chest constricted as if he couldn't get a breath, and his erection strained against his jeans, more than ready to answer the call of her provocative statement.

She was writing about *him* in that book of hers. She wanted him.

Sexually.

Hell, she couldn't have spelled it out any more clearly.

But despite the green lights flashing, and the warm woman an inch away, he would not let himself have her. Not now. Not this way.

Because his brain told him it was a bad idea. She needed to write the book—needed *him*—because someone else had hurt her.

Acknowledging that was the only thing keeping the rest of him in check.

"I can't begin to guess what you must be thinking

of me right now," Miranda admitted quietly, picking at the purple flower sticker on one of her nails.

Making him realize he'd better man up in a hurry if he didn't want to lose any chance he had with her down the road.

"Honestly?" He ground his teeth together and hoped for the best. "It's like wrestling a wildfire, trying to stop myself from doing all the things I want to do with you, to you."

"Oh?" She bit her lip and looked surprised. He cursed his bluntness, but—thankfully—did so inside his head. "Care to elaborate?"

"I'm burning up all over the place." He took a deep breath and deliberately removed his hands from her warm, delectable body. "But I'm telling myself that waiting is the best thing. Give us both a little time to get our heads around what's happening."

Her smile was sweetly grateful, a reminder of what a jackass he would have to be to act on the brain-numbing desire he still felt for her.

"If you need more time to be comfortable with where this is going, I understand." She twined her fingers through the fringe of that throw blanket and stood. "Maybe it would help if I wrote what was going to happen next."

"Sorry?" Damien knew he wasn't thinking clearly, since most of the blood flow had vacated his brain the moment he sat down on the steps with her in the first place. But still…he had no clue what she meant. The flames crackled in the hearth, a log shifting and sending up sparks.

That wasn't the only thing on fire.

"It might help me to write about…" She pointed back and forth between them. "What happens next with the characters in my book. It'll give me time to think about it and look forward to it, so I'm not nervous and weird."

"You're going to write about us being together…before we're together?" If she could only see the video footage running nonstop in his brain, she'd have a full color feature film to work from for inspiration.

He looked up at her from his place on the stairs, since a move toward her—if only to stand up—wouldn't be wise right now. Any momentum in her direction would lead to him touching her. He was dying for another taste of her lips.

"You think I'm crazy, don't you?"

"Are you kidding? I can't wait to read what you come up with." He tugged on the loose end of the blanket that hung around her knees. He hadn't meant to reach toward her, but at least he'd stopped himself before he dragged her to him for another kiss.

She shifted from one foot to the other. "I don't know if I can let you read it."

"As long as I get to live it, Miranda, I'm going to be happy as hell." Hearing the uncertainty in her voice made him more convinced than ever that waiting was the right thing to do. It also made him more than a little protective of her.

"Oh." She hugged her arms around herself, drawing the blanket so tight he could see the outline of all her lean curves. "In that case I'd better get started." A wicked glint came into her eyes. "The sooner I get it written, the sooner it will happen."

"Is that how it works?" He enjoyed seeing her like this. Happy. Excited. Her cheeks flushed pink, confidence radiating from her in spite of her concerns about being awkward.

"I'm new to this, but yes. I think it is." She waited there for a moment, staring at him. "No good-night kiss for inspiration?"

Was she purposely trying to kill him?

"I'm hoping you've got all the inspiration you can handle." Damn it, he'd be cold showering straight through to dawn at this rate. "Because I'm still wrestling that wildfire over here, remember?"

"Right." She nodded. "Sorry." Turning on her heel, she hurried up the steps away from him. "I'll write fast. And if you see a flash drive lying around anywhere, will you let me know? I had one in the laptop when I left L.A. and I can't find it now. I definitely wouldn't want anyone else seeing my story."

"I'll tell the cleaning crew to keep an eye out for it when they come in."

"Thanks." She sauntered off in a billow of blanket.

He stared into the fire from his spot on the steps long after she'd closed her bedroom door with a soft click. He had no idea how he'd survive until she was ready to be with him—not after a kiss that had just about blown his mind. But he would hold back if it killed him, because he wasn't a scumbag like her sister's ex.

And on that note...cool reason returned. Damien planned to find out whatever he could about this guy, because no way in hell was that creep getting any-where near Miranda again.

I HADN'T GOTTEN my good-night kiss then, but I had a whole lot more to think about the next night as I slid between the sheets in one of Damien's empty guest rooms. He had left the farm earlier in the day to check out a mare he was thinking of purchasing, so I had seen him only briefly. Just long enough to exchange some secretive smiles between his chores and the little jobs I'd opted to do to help out—like delivering homemade bread and tea to the Whitemans so they'd have it when they returned from touring a local winery. Violet had left me a note about wanting to get together afterward, but I'd jotted a reply that I had some errands, and maybe Monday would work for me.

I wasn't looking forward to talking about *Gutsy Girl,* and I knew from her visit to Damien the other night that she was anxious for a photo op. Ugh.

I'd also made personal-sized quiches for any Fraser Farm employees I could find during the day. It wouldn't hurt for word of my cooking prowess to spread. And yes, I was well aware that I was ingratiating myself to the staff so maybe some of them would champion my plan to buy the farm stand and convert it to a tearoom. But I don't think anyone who tried my quiche today would complain about my techniques.

Now I wanted to write more of my book, so I could move closer to being with Damien. I opened my laptop to work on my manuscript, just as I'd promised him I would the night before.

Stepping into the fictional world felt like a way to be with Damien without risking too much yet. And I was *dying* to be closer to him. Memories of that kiss lit me up from the inside out, until all I could think about were his hands on me.

Too bad I had to give him over to sexy, confident Shaelynn first. But I knew it was safer to put my heroine with him before I took the chance myself. She could be my avatar. I just wanted to kind of…watch and see what happened. If that made me voyeuristic—or a chicken of the first order—that was okay. I picked up where I'd left off, once I'd gone back through the novel to tweak the stranger's name:

*…arching into D's hand, Shaelynn moaned with the pleasure of his touch. He leaned in to kiss her, capturing the sounds she made with his lips while he knelt beside the tub. Forceful rivulets awakened a new heat inside her, her skin tingling with a hot shiver. Her nipples pebbled to tight peaks as she imagined D. joining her in the tub. Covering her. Settling between her thighs with muscular hips…*

Oh. Yes.

Imagining him in the tub was nice. But wouldn't it be even nicer if he actually joined her there? I tapped my chin and stared off into space, envisioning what it would be like. Then again, I didn't have to *completely* rely on my imagination. Damien just happened to have a huge hot tub downstairs.

Could I go hop in the heated spa and let myself be

creatively inspired? Plus, the hot tub would help me relax. The luxuries that were a part of Damien's world had never been part of mine, so a soak among the jets would be an unprecedented treat.

Grabbing a towel and a hair clip, I carried them down to the spa, balancing them on my laptop. I wasn't sure when Damien would be home, but I would get as much written as quickly as I could. I just hoped he didn't mind me invading his space downstairs.

Not that I was headed into the master suite or anything, even though I'd seen a killer hot tub in there when I'd first explored the house. But there was also an indoor spa area in the lowest level, where the house had been built into a hillside. The back wall of windows looked out over a patio, pool and some scenic pastures. The space had a small bar and a game room decorated in rough-hewn woods lacquered smooth. Pendant lighting over the bar cast enough light on the hot tub. Steam wafted up as I toed the cover off, but the temperature wasn't quite as hot as I wanted, so I flipped a nearby switch and waited for the water to warm up.

Setting my things down on the glazed redbrick surrounding the tub, I skimmed off my clothes and wrapped the thick Turkish terry cloth robe from my room around me, the plush cotton soft against my skin. I could have dug through my belongings to find a swimsuit, but I was writing an *erotic* story. Shaelynn hadn't slid into that tub with her suit on and neither would I. She didn't need to have all the fun first every single time. Tonight, she had Damien's hands on her and I was going to be right there with her, imagining what it was like.

Stepping into the tub, I loosened my robe and let it fall down my shoulders. I kept the hem out of the water while I worked the rest of the cloth lower and lower. Thick steam rose off the water now that the heater had kicked in. I wriggled my toes in the bubbles and slid the robe the rest of the way off while I sank into the inviting warmth.

"Yes-s-s." Silky heat enveloped me, and I hit the buttons for the jets and bubbles, increasing their speed and force. Grabbing the clip, I secured my hair.

Powerful surges of hot water soothed my muscles beneath the surface, while smaller bubbles burst near my nose like a tubful of champagne. I reclined on one of the built-in seats and let the magic happen. The sensations were hot, sensuous and entirely decadent.

Especially with snippets of my novel still running around in my head. How ironic was it that I'd started out writing a story about Shaelynn alone and lost in the woods when a gorgeous stranger found her. And the very next day, I broke down in the SUV, only to be rescued by Damien? I couldn't shake the sense that my book was coming to life, which made it feel all the more daring to keep writing.

I soaked in the heat for a while, inhaling steam and letting the stress of the past months float away. When my heart rate dropped a few notches, my whole body relaxing, I dried my hands on my robe so I could use my laptop. I picked up with the story right where I'd left off.

*...Her nipples tightened to peaks as D broke their kiss and took one taut bud into his mouth. She didn't know*

*what had come over her to let him touch her this way, but there was no turning back now. Not with her body on fire and her thoughts consumed with images of him. Covering her. Settling between her thighs with muscular hips. In response, she widened her legs to make room for him. And, perhaps, to feel the forceful rush of water over her sensitive sex.*

*"You could come in," she urged, reaching one wet hand up to his collar to shove aside his coat. "Join me."*

*He sat back on his heels to observe her in the moonlight, a veil of steam rising between them. Would he strip off his clothes and fulfill her fantasies?*

*"I like watching you." His voice wrapped around her like a seductive spell. "Why don't you show me what you're feeling?"*

*Confused, she blinked through the fog of awareness and tugged on his hand. Drawing him near. But instead of touching her, he reached into the tub and turned a jet nozzle toward her breast, unleashing a torrent across the tip of one nipple.*

*Caught in the sensual onslaught, she felt her eyes slide shut as she let the pleasure take her.*

*Her body ached and her sex pulsed with need. She cupped her breasts, craving more.*

*D's whispered encouragement in her ear let her know this was what he wanted. To watch. To see her succumb to the need. Imagining his hand on her, she slipped one palm beneath the water's surface, gliding a fingertip over the delicate folds between her thighs. She gasped.*

*"You look so beautiful." D's breath was warm*

*against her cheek as he leaned to kiss the curve of her neck where it met her shoulder.*

*Shaelynn arched deeper into the bench seat and lifted her hips, making it easier to repeat the seductive touch. It didn't take much. The barest brush of her finger combined with the rush of water took her higher. She tossed her head back and forth, sensation coiling tight. Anticipation building.*

*Water pounded her body in hot streams, intensifying the feelings. Her breath came hard and fast, until she panted with the effort of holding back her release. All along, he whispered in her ear, his voice anchoring her in the sensation, urging her with wicked promises of other pleasures to come. Sighing his name with a pent-up breath, she drew two fingers along her sex. Imagined herself looking into his eyes as he sheathed himself with her. Pushed his hips into hers until he was buried heart-deep within her.*

*"Oh!" A startled cry burst from her lips as her orgasm hit her.*

*She gripped the sides of the tub, wishing she held D's broad shoulders in her hands instead. Wave after wave of pleasure shook through her, wringing a satisfied moan from her even as she wanted much, much more....*

I had to stop a minute, my fingers poised above the keyboard and my heart pumping faster while I savored what had happened. Shaelynn hadn't gotten any closer to making love with "D" than I had, her orgasm brought on by pleasuring herself while thinking of his hands on her.

But oh…she wanted more. And so did I. I could feel the blood coursing through my veins, heating my skin everywhere. The tension deep within me tightened. Heightened. I felt restless with this ache for more. So much so, I wasn't sure if I could keep writing.

Deep in thought, I jerked as a footstep on the stairs caught me off guard.

"Miranda?" a sexy, masculine voice called—the same one that had just coaxed my heroine to lose all her inhibitions. "Are you down there?"

Damien was home.

Nervousness twined with excitement. Hunger.

He'd paused on the stairway, waiting for my answer. No doubt he'd heard the hot-tub jets and come to investigate. It said a lot about him that he didn't just barge into the game room while I was in the spa. He knew that I wanted to take things slow, and he respected that, even though he'd made it clear he was ready for more than I was.

My heart beat like a jackhammer, my whole body tense with nerves and—yes—sexual excitement. I wanted him even though I was so nervous I was shaking.

"Yes," I called finally, knowing I would be okay with a guy who could rein himself in enough to wait on the stairs for my reply. "You can come down."

I pushed away from the laptop, but didn't close it. Settling into a seat on the far side of the tub, I allowed myself the simple pleasure of watching him come down the stairs and cross the floor toward me.

His hazel eyes never left me, locked with mine like

a guided missile. He appeared exactly as I'd imagined him in my story, that intense gaze of his making my insides simmer with awareness. The strong lines of his face, the aristocratic high cheekbones and chiseled, workingman's jaw, were features I could picture perfectly when I closed my eyes or when I wrote about him. I'd spent a lot of time staring. Memorizing.

Enjoying.

"You're back," I observed, lightly trailing my fingertips over the soft, breaking bubbles at the surface. "I hope you don't mind me making myself at home."

My voice sounded awkward, as if it belonged to someone else. My heart beat wildly. Dressed in a light blue shirt with a gray-and-yellow tie he'd loosened enough that a T-shirt showed beneath, he looked good enough to eat. He stood at the edge of the tub, his breath coming hard as he studied me.

"Let me put it this way." His voice was low. His jaw clenched with tension. "If I was the one writing the book, I don't think I could have thought up a scene this good."

DAMIEN KNEW HE SHOULDN'T have walked down those steps to the lower level. He'd recognized as much the second the scent of chlorine hit his nose, understanding damn well that Miranda must have made use of the spa.

Now his blood ran hot in his veins at the sight of her glistening bare shoulders above the churning water. Locks of her short, newly colored hair clung in wet waves to her neck, even though she had most of it caught in a clip. A delicate silver chain around her neck reflected the light as she moved.

She had to be naked.

The discarded robe off to one side said as much as that bare shoulder. He couldn't look anywhere else, seized with the desire to lick a droplet of water from her skin where it rolled down her arm.

"Actually, I came down here just for that reason—so it would be a good scene." She pointed toward her laptop, an open document visible on the screen.

And? Had she written it yet? He hated to rush her. Would not rush her, damn it. But there she was. Naked. In his hot tub.

He forced himself to sit on the edge of the lacquered bricks surrounding the spa. Close, but not too close. He tried not to stare down into the water, where the tops of her breasts were occasionally visible. Okay, maybe he didn't try that hard.

"How is it turning out so far?" With any luck, her heroine had already overcome her doubts and ripped off the hero's clothes.

Tension threaded through his muscles. Tightened every inch of him.

"Um…" Color rose in her cheeks. "I think there's an interesting phenomenon at work."

A multi-orgasmic phenomenon, he hoped. Or an insatiable sexual craving that he'd have to work all night to satisfy. He was very ready to provide whatever she needed.

"How so?" He ground the question out between clenched teeth, glancing toward the laptop. He wasn't

sure he'd be able to read what she wrote without…
Hell. He was already so wound up he could barely see
straight.

"I was—" her gaze darted to his "—highly inspired.
But I ended up… That is, my *heroine* wound up with a
self-gratification scene."

He wanted to think his way through what that meant.
For Miranda. For them. But his brain stalled on an
image of her touching herself, and remained right there.

Any attempt to reassure her—to say anything at
all—ended in a dry rasp from his throat. Sweat beaded
on his forehead from the effort to stay still. Not reach
for her.

"Crazy, right?" She gave a small shrug that lifted her
left breast perilously close to the surface of the water.
"But I think—subconsciously—I don't want my heroine to be with you before I am."

Silence hung in the room for long moments after that
announcement. He tried to silence the buzz in his head
so he could make sense of her words. But he didn't trust
his first instinct, which told him she'd just flashed him
the go-ahead sign.

"I've had a tough time staying focused, with you sitting so close and so naked." He felt his right temple start
to throb. "Which means I'm going to ask that you…"
He scraped a hand over his face, hoping that closing his
eyes for a second would erase the image of her from the
backs of his eyelids. "I need you to be very, very clear
about what you want."

"Right." She nodded, her brow furrowed. "I'm not
going to be able to write my way through this scene, and

I don't want to decide what happens next." Her cheeks flushed darker and her lips trembled a little bit. "I just want you to touch me."

# 6

I SHUT DOWN my issues.

It wasn't easy, but it was eas*ier* than it had ever been before. I tuned out the part of my brain that said I wasn't good enough or pretty enough or deserving of this man. Instead, I focused on the heat in his eyes and reminded myself of how patient he'd already been with me. How kind. How honest. This moment was a long time coming for me, and the time was right.

Damien was *right.*

I could tell from the way his eyes lightened and then darkened that he definitely wanted me. And I was definitely ready for more. I'd known it the whole time I'd been writing that scene where Shaelynn dreamed of Damien touching her. I just flat-out had not wanted to let her have him first. I'd been saving this moment for me.

His shirt came off in a blur of burnished muscle and gray poplin. The tie, the shirt, the tee beneath it...all gone. He stared at me with an unmistakable glint in his hazel eyes. He wanted me badly. But he had every intention of treating me right.

My skin got goose bumps under the water. Pleasure spun through me just beneath the skin, sending my nerves on high alert. My breasts beaded so tight they ached, and my thighs pressed against a heat that didn't have anything to do with the hot tub.

"Don't. Move." He backed away, ducking into the adjacent bathroom. I heard drawers open and bang closed again.

When he reappeared, he had an armful of fluffy white towels and a handful of silver foil packets that he tossed on the decking around the tub.

"Condoms. A lot of them." I said it aloud, just because the whole encounter felt surreal. I wasn't sure if I wanted it to feel like a fantasy. Or 100 percent reality.

A little of both, maybe.

I did not want to mess this up.

"I figured I'd be very, very clear about what I want, too." He gave me a pirate's grin—all white teeth and wickedness. "But I understand if those condoms are just wishful thinking on my part. Better to have them and not need them than to…"

"Yeah." I nodded. "I get it. Easier to stay in the mood if we've got them nearby." I remembered how I froze last time when he wanted to move from the staircase to a bedroom. This way, if things got heated, we could stay in the moment.

I could keep my insecurities at bay.

"You can still write the scene to play out however you want, Miranda," he assured me. "You're in charge."

I shook my head. "My imagination isn't this good."

My breath caught. A shiver ran through me. I could never have written this. Him. Imagining that gorgeous, hard body of his all over me was easy. But I would never have guessed the prelude. The lead-in. The way his eyes smoldered as he unfastened his pants.

My eyes dropped south, drawn by the sight of what was going on beneath the belt.

"All for me," I whispered, half to myself and half to the part of me that was Shaelynn.

I was pretty sure that she was cheering me on from somewhere deep in my subconscious. No matter how nervous I was, I had the heart of a gutsy girl, damn it.

Damien had the rest of his clothes off before I could blink, his thick erection jutting from between his hips. I think maybe he was giving me time to get used to the idea of being with him. The condoms. The nakedness. He was giving me a last chance to bail out if I needed it.

Apparently he didn't realize how committed I was to this program.

"Please hurry," I urged, reaching wet arms toward him. Once he kissed me, I'd be okay.

He dropped onto the edge of the tub just as I arched up. He slid into the water and I shifted onto his lap. His arms wrapped around me, the raw strength of him obvious even as he held me gently.

Sensations bombarded me, from the tickle of hair on his thighs along mine to the musky, male scent of his warm skin. I looked up into his hazel eyes for a second before his mouth landed on mine and he kissed me.

My breasts flattened against his chest, the peaks

beading and aching. I cupped his chin and cradled his face, craving every angle of the kiss imaginable, wanting to eat him up. Tension coiled inside me, a flagrant, hot awareness of him. But he moved slowly, teasing my mouth with purposeful swipes of his tongue, nipping my lower lip with his teeth and making me gasp with sharp pangs of want.

"I want this," I said aloud, making sure he knew it. I'd been waiting for so long to have this kind of kiss. "I want you."

He broke the contact, his eyes boring into mine while the steam from the hot tub swirled around us, sealing us together in a white veil.

"I dreamed about this," he confided, fingers splayed along my spine.

"Me, too." Since before I even met him. Although the dreams had gotten far more specific and tantalizing since Damien gave my sensual imaginings a definite focus.

"You're shaking," he noted, cupping my face in his palm, angling my chin so he could see into my eyes in the reflected lights from overhead.

"That's not normal?" I shifted on his thighs, edging closer to his hips and nudging the hard length between them.

He ground his teeth and sucked in a breath, making me realize how much what I did affected him. What amazing, powerful knowledge. I tucked it away deep in my mind, grateful to him for that gift. His fingers played lightly on my cheek, traveled up into my hair.

"Just making sure we're good." His words cracked

on a dry note, making me realize how much he held back for my sake.

I took a deep breath, certain I wanted this. Him.

"I'm great. Better than great." I traced his lips with one finger, finding his mouth surprisingly soft compared with the rest of him. My gaze followed the damp trail I left behind, the water glistening until I leaned down to lick it off.

Growing bolder, I tugged his lower lip between my teeth and nipped it. His shaft twitched against my hip and I wondered if it was too soon to sit astride him. I'd been ready for him since he'd walked into the room, but I didn't want to rush.

Then again, I didn't want to give myself time to panic....

"Stay with me," he whispered between kisses. "Let me taste you again."

He kissed me hard, his lips settling on mine with a hungry possessiveness that made me weak in my knees and chased away the worries again. His arms held me captive, positioning me where he wanted while he had his way with my mouth. A languid desire gave way to something more frenzied. More hungry. I pressed closer, my breasts aching and sensitive. The warm wall of male muscle provided the best abrasion I could imagine. I was more shameless than Shaelynn as I wrapped my arms around Damien's neck and held on, needing more and more of this feeling.

He pulled back and paused for a second to watch me. Maybe he was satisfied with what he saw, because he didn't stop. He lowered his lips to my neck and I moaned at the sensation. Water bubbled at my back. His tongue licked sexy pathways down my throat, then down my chest, where my breasts rose out of the water. Suddenly, I ached there with a fierceness unlike anything I'd ever felt before. I needed his kiss *there*. Now.

"Please," I murmured, threading my fingers through his hair while the bubbles simmered all around us. "I'm crawling out of my skin."

He cupped a breast in his palm and lowered his mouth to capture the tip. My eyes stayed glued on him, hypnotized by the sight. White teeth flashed for an instant before he drew on the crest. Hard. I bucked against him, twisting to get a better feel of his body. This was what I had been craving for years without knowing it. This tender attention. A man caring about what I felt and what I wanted. Needed.

Right now, I wanted him all over me. Between my thighs. My sex ached for him.

Visions of my novel ran through my head. Damien's voice in my ear urged me on. I think that's what gave me courage to straddle him now. I shifted my body so I sat astride him, my knees planted on a built-in tub bench so that my sex met the thick erection that awaited me.

He lifted his head, his eyes greener than I'd ever seen them, the pupils dilated wide.

"I need to taste you first."

I was still thinking about what that meant when he reached for a handful of the fluffy towels he'd brought out to the spa. Blankly, I watched as he leaned over me and around me to spread the towels on the edge of the hot tub.

Before I could ask, he lifted me from the water and laid me on the bed of terry cloth, my legs still dangling over the edge of the spa.

"What—"

My unspoken question was answered when he knelt on the bench, positioning himself between my legs, my knees propped on his broad shoulders.

"Oh. *Oh*."

Any awkwardness vanished as he took me in his mouth and kissed me. My eyes slid closed, the carnality of seeing his strong torso between my thighs almost too much for my overwrought senses to bear. The sensations spiraling from the feel of his tongue on my swollen sex were all I could handle right now. It felt very decadent. Very naughty. And better than anything I could have imagined in my feeble writer's imagination.

"Damien." It felt so good to say his name. To know that he was the one who kissed me intimately.

I thrashed against the towels, my skin cooling from the drying water even as another heat burned me up inside.

He increased the pressure, responding to needs I never voiced, as if he knew exactly what I wanted long before I did. I gripped fistfuls of towel in each hand, holding on for dear life. Anchoring myself to this moment and grounding myself in the reality of it. Damien Fraser kissed me. Licked me.

Suckled me...

I flew apart so hard and fast that I screamed aloud. Waves of pleasure rocked me, pounding through my feminine muscles with delectable intensity. I writhed against the floor and against Damien, my legs twitching, but he never relinquished his hold on me, urging me higher with a few final devastating flicks of his talented tongue.

My breath gone, my senses stunned, I was grateful when he levered himself up to wrap me in his strong arms. He kissed my shoulder. My neck. Nipped my ear while the aftershocks continued to fire through me.

"Are you okay?" he asked gruffly, his concern as evident as his hunger.

My heart melted for this amazing man, and I fell a little more for him even as I knew I probably shouldn't.

"Way better than okay," I managed to reply with an effort. I kissed his cheek, unable to process all the things going through my brain, even as the pleasure still coursed through my body. The way Damien made me feel really hammered home how thoroughly I'd been deceived as a naive teen. Sex was so much more amazing than I ever could have guessed. And technically, we hadn't even had it yet. I smiled. "I don't think I have words for how that felt."

A very male grin told me he liked that answer.

"Ready for more?" he asked, his voice practically a growl.

And yes, mine was practically a purr. Mind-blowing satisfaction apparently could do that to a woman.

"I thought you'd never ask."

His hands shook.

Damien almost couldn't believe it when he saw his

fingers tremble as he smoothed aside Miranda's hair and kissed her. Partly that tremor was from holding back. But he'd be fooling himself if he thought that was the only reason. This thing happening between them was about a whole lot more than sex.

His feelings for her were growing faster than he could deal with them. And he hadn't even been inside her yet. Ignoring the implications of that, since he was in no position to think about it now, Damien focused on what mattered.

Her.

"Are you warm enough?" He ran a hand up her silky thigh. Her skin had cooled while he'd pleasured her, and he didn't want anything distracting her from what was about to happen.

He needed her totally in the moment with him.

"I'm plenty warm, thanks to you," she teased, rocking her hips against his as she reached for the condom stash on the tub deck.

He ground his teeth together, willing himself to go slow. To take his time. He didn't intend to get so caught up in what he wanted that he lost sight of what she needed. He wanted to blot out every memory of the bastard who'd hurt her.

"But if any part of this gets chronicled in fiction, I want it to be just right." He figured it would be better to keep the moment light, to help her focus on him and not think about the past.

"Fiction will favor you, Damien Fraser." She grinned and ran her hands up and down his arms while he rolled on a condom. "In fact, I know a certain writer who will sing your praises in lavish prose that will make other women long to meet you."

"I've got the woman I want to meet," he admitted as he sheathed himself, then kissed her.

She sighed in his arms, wrapping herself around him and letting him take over. For just a moment, he allowed himself to look at her, her eyes closed and her features relaxed while he kissed her.

Miranda Cortland was so beautiful. Earrings studded the rim of her ear. Tattooed eyeliner stamped both eyelids. But neither distracted him from the delicate loveliness beneath. She could wear all the flower stickers she wanted on her nails. All the crazy clothes. He'd still see the vulnerable sweetness bolstered by steely determination. A woman who'd found a way to overcome old hurts and find a new life for herself.

The need to protect her threatened to steal the moment, so he gave her the only thing he could. Steadying her thighs, he reached between them to tease the tender bud of her sex. Reawaken the heat he'd kindled earlier. Her eyes flew open, locking on his while her lips rounded on a breathy gasp.

He took her mouth with his, claiming a kiss. To his surprise, she trailed a tentative touch up the ridge of his shaft, setting off a reaction so strong that sweat popped along his forehead. He couldn't hold back.

Hooking an arm around her waist, he lifted her against him. Positioned her right where he needed her. He entered her gently, carefully. He guessed it had been a long time for her.

He hadn't anticipated how much she wanted him. So

when her legs locked around his waist and she thrust her hips forward, he had to bite his tongue to hold himself in check.

Focusing on the sound of the bubbling water behind them, instead of the sweet, needy noises she made in the back of her throat, Damien waited until he had control of himself before he moved again. Guided her hips back and forth in a slow rhythm with his.

Her nails dug lightly into his shoulders, her head thrown back, putting her breasts right at mouth level. He traced circles around one pink tip, making the bud tighten to pebbly hardness. He drew on her, lavishing one full breast with attention and then the other. Increasing the rhythm, he felt himself losing control. Her fingers raked through his hair. Her thighs clenched him tight. She met him thrust for thrust, as lost to the moment as he felt.

When a ragged cry left her lips, he felt the first pulses of her sex around him. Her release set off his own, their shouts mingling above the drone of the hot tub. He fell into her, spent, even as the contractions kept milking a response from him. He came and came, powerless to the sensations that drained him dry. Hell, he probably would have collapsed on her if Miranda hadn't held him tight, her slender arms steadying him with surprising strength.

Holy. Crap.

He couldn't think. Couldn't speak. Damn near couldn't see straight. It took time for his breath to return, along with awareness of anything besides Miranda and the incredible way she made him feel.

"I'm taking you upstairs," he announced, rolling to one side. He reached for more towels—fresh, dry ones—to wrap her in.

At her sweetly compliant nod, he couldn't help but smile. If he asked her to move in with him or let him take care of her, would she agree as easily?

He guessed not. But right now, he was just happy as hell to have her in his house and on her way to his bed.

# 7

I'D NEVER WOKEN UP in a man's bed before.

Sunlight streamed over my face and arms, my limbs tangled with white sheets from the time Damien had awoken me in the middle of the night and we... A smile stole over my face as I tried to remember all the incredible highlights from the night before. Being with him—every time—had been amazing. Instead of feeling like a failure, I felt like a seduction superhero. Call me the Orgasm Queen.

Of course, I have no idea if I was any good in bed. But Damien had enough sexual smarts for both of us, apparently. Besides, it was impossible to question myself now, when I still felt so freaking amazing.

"You look happy." A voice came from behind me on the king-size mattress. A sexy, rough, he-man voice that had filled my dreams in the few stolen hours of sleep I'd had.

"How can you tell?" I turned to peer far enough over my shoulder to see that he faced me. His eyes were open, his jaw shadowed with dark stubble that made him look even more like a sexy pirate.

Immediately, I had another idea for a story. One that involved a lot of bodice ripping and a great deal of ravishing. This one would be better than anything I'd saved on that flash drive, but even so, I'd feel better if I found it.

Damien lifted a hand to my face and smoothed his fingers along my jaw.

"I've been watching you wake up. When I saw your cheekbone lift, right here—" he brushed it with his thumb "—I knew you were smiling."

"Hmm." I turned into his arms, battling a small stab of insecurity about my body. I could be thin the rest of my life and never get over that flash of instinct to hide myself. "You were watching me without me knowing. I hope you enjoyed the view."

"Enjoy it? Lady, I can't get enough." A heavy hand spanned my waist on top of the sheet, and my body came to life right away. Awareness pricked along my bare arms and down to the tops of my breasts, barely covered by the sheet.

I slipped my knee between his, marveling at the heated warmth of him.

"Me, either," I whispered as I pressed kisses to his chest. It was too soon to think about what last night had meant. Maybe if we stayed in bed all day, we wouldn't have to think about it.

Or talk about it.

The doorbell rang, however, before I could kiss him as much as I wanted.

We separated enough to exchange glances. I knew we were both thinking about the foal. He was new enough for us to still worry about his health.

"You can stay here," Damien assured me, when I hopped out of bed after him.

"That's okay." I slid into his bathrobe, since my own clothes were nowhere near. "I'd just eavesdrop to make sure everything's okay."

He chuckled softly while he pulled on a pair of jeans, commando. Now I'd be thinking about how naked he was under that denim.

"Maybe it's Violet Whiteman?" He moved toward a set of blinds covering the massive windows that wrapped one side of the master suite. "Did she ever catch up with you yesterday?"

Nerves tightened my gut while I tied the sash on the heavy, Turkish terry cloth robe. I didn't want to think about my old life intruding here on my new happiness.

"I dropped off some tea and bread for them while they were touring a local winery. I guess Violet writes some kind of blog about wine." I peered over Damien's broad shoulder as he held aside the blinds. "I'll admit I timed my stop at their suite when I was certain I'd miss them."

He pointed to a large white vehicle almost directly below where we were standing. "You know anyone with a white Cadillac?"

"Joelle!" I squealed, and squeezed his arm.

"The tea shop owner?" He let go of the blinds as the bell chimed again.

"Yes." I hurried toward the door. "Do you mind if I go answer it?"

"Of course not." He didn't follow me. "I'll probably hit the shower and check on Stretch. Let you two visit."

"Okay. Thanks." I hit the hallway and took the stairs two at a time, shouting, "Coming!"

Skidding to a halt in front of the huge double doors at the front of the house, I grabbed a wrought-iron ring and pulled open one of the oak behemoths that made me feel like Alice in Wonderland during her small phase.

"Joelle!" My girlfriend and former boss stood on the welcome mat with arms folded and toe tapping.

She quit tapping when she saw it was me. With her shoulder-length brown hair worn in a flip, she looked like an artsy Stepford wife, or maybe a cross between Martha Stewart and Zooey Deschanel. At the tearoom she normally wore floral aprons over an all-black uniform of a pencil skirt and silk blouse. Today, she'd ditched her normal clothes for a T-shirt and jeans covered by a knee-length gray cardigan sweater. Her white Cadillac had been pulled up to the front step, parked squarely in front of the doors as if she'd planned to stay for only a second.

"Miranda?" Her amber eyes landed on my hair, her freckles visible in the morning sunlight, since she wore no makeup except for long, fake eyelashes. A diamond stud winked just below one eyebrow. "What on earth did you do to your hair?"

Before I could answer, she reached for my sleeve and gripped a handful of white Turkish terry cloth.

"And what are you wearing?" she asked, staring at me as if I'd dropped out of the sky from another planet.

"What does it look like?" I teased, and crossed the threshold to hug her. "Is that any way to greet a friend?"

She hugged me hard until I tugged her inside and shut the door.

"Sorry. I've been worried about you." As she stood back, she peered past the foyer into the heart of the house. "But you look like you've made yourself at home here." She gave me a sly grin and a wink.

"How did you find me?" Joelle hadn't said anything about checking up on me so soon. I'd left only on Friday, and here she was, late Monday morning.

"You told me you were visiting the farm stand on the Fraser Farm property when you texted me Thursday night, don't you remember?" She wrapped the sweater tighter around herself and then ran a hand over a heavy Mexican-style armoire in the hall. "You sounded like it was a sure thing."

"I vaguely remember." I motioned her toward the kitchen. "You'll notice this isn't the farm stand."

"No kidding. But you've been ignoring my messages all weekend. I visited my aunt in San Francisco yesterday and thought I'd check things out for myself, so I could see if you needed a hand getting settled."

"To help or to spy on me?" I pulled a pub stool out from under a table in the dining area and waved for her to take a seat.

She didn't. She roamed around the breakfast bar as I found mugs, spoons and tea bags in a sideboard covered with coffee paraphernalia.

"A little of both," she confessed, her platform heels tapping softly along the marble tiles. "I drove around that empty old farm stand building and some young guy mending fences along the road told me you might be at the 'big house.' So I kept going until I found a big house."

"Sorry, I haven't been checking my phone." Lighting the flame under a heavy stainless-steel kettle, I started heating the water.

Sunlight poured in the windows along the back of the house, bathing us in warmth even though the sheen of dew on the trees outside told me it was cool today. The kitchen had high ceilings with exposed beams that looked as if they came from ancient redwoods, they were so large. Stainless-steel appliances and a six-burner cooktop had made it a fun kitchen to bake in the day before. Everything in here seemed brand-new, as if a decorator had outfitted it but no one ever used it.

"Here." Joelle pulled a small square tin from her pocket. "Try this."

I smiled, recognizing the containers she used to sell her tearoom's special blends.

"I don't know if there's a tea ball." Still, I opened the tin and inhaled, recognizing the spicy mix of cinnamon, vanilla and about ten other herbs, a tea she marketed as "Holiday Escape."

"You're kidding. What is this? The Stone Age?" She tsked and opened a few cabinets and drawers. Finally, she handed me a small strainer. "Use this and start talking, sister. What are you doing, sleeping in the big house and wearing a man's bathrobe four sizes too big for you?"

"Er..." I hoped the teakettle would boil and save me from the third degree. "I plead the Fifth?"

Joelle shrugged out of her sweater and perched on one of the stools at the breakfast bar.

"Not an option." She positioned her cell phone nearby on the granite, and double-checked that her ringer was silent, a habit she'd had as long as I'd known her. She was too ladylike to let a sound disturb her tea, and too business savvy to ignore important calls.

I'd learned a lot about being an entrepreneur from her. I hoped it was enough to help me run my own tearoom.

"Okay." I wondered how much to say. I trusted Joelle, but the relationship—could I call it that?—with Damien was so new I didn't know how to describe it, let alone how I felt about it. "I'm staying here a few days while the owner of the property considers whether or not to sell me the farm stand."

"He invited you to stay with him while he thinks about it?" Her arched eyebrow let me know exactly what she thought of my half answers. "And opened his wardrobe to you in the process?"

"He's a very nice man." I couldn't hide a smile as the teakettle whistled and I poured the water through the herbs in the strainer.

"I'll bet." Snorting, she drummed her fingernails on the countertop. "I've tried to set you up on dates. Hot guys have propositioned you at the tearoom. And not once since I've known you have you given a man the time of day. Yet you're here for a weekend and…"

She gave my bathrobe a meaningful glare.

"I'm trying to get past some old issues, right?" I'd told Joelle about Rick. About writing the erotic novel as a way to move past the hang-ups he'd left me with. She and I had been friends ever since she'd hired me. "And this guy who owns the place—Damien—walks straight out of the pages of my book."

Frowning, she took her cup from me and removed the strainer basket so I could use it for mine.

"Are you telling me he swept you off your feet?"

"Not exactly." Although everything had happened so fast, maybe there had been some sweeping involved. "But he definitely was a white knight to my damsel in distress when the Highlander gave out on Highway 1."

"Didn't I tell you to get a tune-up before you left?"

I wish I'd at least had the lock fixed before I made the trip. Bad enough I'd broken down. I hated the thought that I'd left all my stuff vulnerable on the side of the road in an unlocked vehicle, while I walked to get help. What if someone had taken my flash drive then? I was missing that *Gutsy Girl* shirt, too. I'd been too busy to really look through all my stuff to see if anything else was unaccounted for.

I poured a fresh spoonful of the dried herbs into the strainer for my tea, enjoying the repetition of an old ritual in my new surroundings. Joelle had brought a little piece of home for me, right down to the familiar scent of the Holiday Escape blend.

"You told me I should get the tune-up, yes. But I didn't. Thankfully, Damien picked me up, plus he towed the Highlander." Maybe it was the Midwest farmer's daughter in me talking, but I could dig a guy with a big truck.

"So he brought you here and sold you the farm stand?" Joelle's bangle bracelets clanged on the counter as she leaned forward. "I didn't see any signs of life down there, but I can help you get set up. I even brought you a few cases of tea so you'd have some starter inventory."

"Really?" Touched, I knew enough about the high end brands she carried to recognize this as a very generous gift. "Wow. Thank you so much. But, actually, I haven't bought the property yet."

"I thought it looked perfect." She took a slow sip of her tea. "Did you have another place in mind?"

"No. I want it." I inhaled the fragrant steam, breathing in some confidence along with it. I could still make the dream happen. I knew it. "Damien is concerned that my reality television fame will bring an unwanted element to the farm."

She pursed her lips. "I'd like to say that sounds snobby of him, but since I couldn't handle all the extra attention the show brought to the tearoom, I guess that would be hypocritical, wouldn't it?"

I laughed. "But it's only natural you'd get more stargazers with a business on Melrose Avenue. How many people are going to make the trek to Northern California wine country for the sake of a reality show winner?" The more I thought about it, the more frustrated it made me. Why wouldn't he give me a chance? "By the time I'm ready to open for business, *Gutsy Girl* will probably be airing with a whole new slate of contestants and I'll be long forgotten."

"I hope so." My friend stared at me, her eyebrows knitting together in a way that made the diamond stud shift.

"You sound worried. If things don't work out here, I'm sure I'll find a good space for the business somewhere." I knew Damien was having the guy who drove the horse trailers take a look at my SUV today to see if he could fix it, so I'd be mobile again soon. Not that I was in any great hurry to leave, given the incredible night Damien and I had spent together.

My breath hitched just thinking about it.

"It's not the business I'm worried about." She pulled out a wrinkled piece of pink paper from the pocket of the sweater hanging over the chair next to her. "Look."

Curious, I unfolded the sheet and saw it was from an old-fashioned message pad printed with "While you were away…" across the top. The kind of pad Joelle stocked beside an equally old-fashioned phone near the kitchen at Melrose Tearoom.

"'Miranda's sister, Nina, called.'" I read the message aloud and waited for it to make sense. "As in *my* sister?"

Nina wouldn't have known where I worked, unless she'd asked our parents. My mother had phoned me at the tearoom a few times over the years, mostly when she wanted to remind me of a family birthday that she thought required me to send presents.

"It's got to be." Joelle bent her head beside mine to read the writing again. "She left her name and everything. One of the guys busing tables wrote this down during the Friday afternoon tea service."

Which meant midafternoon, right when I'd been walking along the highway getting sunburned by the winter rays.

"I haven't heard from Nina in six years." I couldn't imagine why she'd call me now. "Unless..."

"What?"

"She could be calling to stir up trouble. Ask for money from the *Gutsy Girl* winnings."

I remembered one time at the county fair when I'd saved my chore money to do the bungee jump because a cute senior boy I was crushing on, Pete Rangel, volunteered at the booth, which raised money for MS. But when I finally worked up the nerve to ask Pete for the bungee jump ticket, I realized that Nina was already at the booth and flirting with him. Amazed that she'd saved up enough money to do the expensive jump, I also discovered my own money was missing. Nina must have taken it. Worse, she'd probably snitched it when she'd fake-hugged me in front of her friends to pretend she wasn't evil.

"The interviews with her Nebraska friends that made it on TV did say both Nina and Rick had spent a lot of money in that divorce," Joelle reminded me.

"My money is going in my sock drawer," I muttered

darkly, still irritated about that long-ago incident. "She knows better than to ask me for anything."

"O-kay." Joelle rolled her eyes, unimpressed with my bluster. "What if she's grown up since she was so awful to you back then? What if she actually had news for you—like her creep of an ex-husband was on his way to L.A.?"

DAMIEN DIDN'T MEAN to eavesdrop.

But the words still hung in the kitchen as he entered to introduce himself.

"Do you have reason to believe Rick is actively looking for Miranda?" He strode over to the breakfast bar, where Miranda sat beside a slender Latina with dark bangs and a sixties-style hairdo. The woman's manicured red nails wrapped around a stoneware mug, and there was a big diamond rock on her left hand.

Someone, somewhere, had wanted a neon sign announcement that this woman was taken.

"That's what I'm worried about." The brunette turned to him and offered her other hand. "I'm Joelle Johnson."

"Damien Fraser." He gave her fingers a squeeze and released her, his arm finding its way around Miranda's back. Tough to make small talk until he'd discovered whatever news Joelle had brought with her. "What makes you think this guy could be headed out here?"

"A message from my sister," Miranda interjected, clutching her mug with both hands. He noticed a few of the stickers on her nails were peeling at the edges.

"Apparently, Nina called the tearoom Friday and left her name. But that's all."

Miranda withdrew a mangled piece of pink paper and smoothed it out on the granite, pressing down the edges.

"See?" She pointed at the note.

"'Miranda's sister, Nina, called,'" he read aloud, frowning. "This is the sister you never talk to?"

"I only have one sibling." Something about the stilted way she said it made him wonder if she was upset. With him? Or with her family situation?

He headed over to the counter to start a pot of coffee, one of the few things he ever used the massive kitchen for.

Joelle cleared her throat. "I was only speculating about what she wanted, but since Nina has never called the tearoom before and has hardly ever called Miranda—"

"Never," Miranda clarified, staring down at the pink message.

"—it seemed like she might have something important to say. And from all accounts, she had an acrimonious parting with the bastard of an ex-husband."

While Damien wondered what "accounts" she'd heard and from where, a sharp knock came at the back door a second before it opened. Footsteps sounded along the hardwood in the screened porch.

"Anybody home?" Scotty called, before opening a second door, between the porch and the kitchen.

Damien waved him in. The farmhand usually

stopped by most workdays to grab a cup of coffee or to share something his wife had baked. Damien's easy rapport with Scotty reminded him of the way Ted had treated him when he'd been running the farm. Damien had always appreciated feeling at home here. He may have doubled the size of the house, but some things he kept just the same.

"Come on in," Miranda said, at the same time he did.

While they exchanged looks at their unexpected chorus, Scotty's eyebrows shot up, his gaze glued to Miranda in a man's bathrobe.

"Sorry if I'm interrupting." Scotty's feet stayed glued to the mat by the door. "I can come back later."

"Don't be silly," she chided, waving him inside. "There are more quiches in the fridge if you want one."

"Quiches?" Damien asked, his stomach rumbling, while Scotty practically sprinted to the side-by-side refrigerator.

"I made a bunch yesterday for your staff," she announced, before turning to Joelle. "I used that recipe for a zucchini, bacon and Gruyère quiche. It was great."

"The spinach and Swiss was my favorite," Scotty called, already manhandling the aluminum foil tins stacked and labeled on one shelf.

Damien left the coffeepot to battle for his share of the leftovers.

"How many kinds did you make?" He turned on the oven even as he tried a bite of the light, flakey crust and amazing egg filling while it was still cold. "Wow."

The doorbell rang before he could mumble anything

else around the mouthful of the best quiche he'd ever eaten. Miranda could seriously cook.

"I so should have gotten dressed," she muttered, sliding off her seat to answer it.

"I can get it." Damien realized his kitchen—damn, his whole house—had never been so full. He hurried to beat her to the door.

"That's okay, I've got it." She waved him off, giving him a sexy wink over one shoulder. "Enjoy your breakfast."

He followed her, anyway. Rumors of that bastard Rick left Damien unsettled, and he wasn't leaving her alone anytime soon.

But when she pulled open the front door, it wasn't a dirtbag former boyfriend standing there.

Petite Violet Whiteman had a point-and-shoot camera in her hand. Aimed right at Miranda.

"Miranda Cortland, why didn't you tell me it was you!" she squealed as she clicked the shutter of her camera. "I had no idea I was visiting with the Nebraska Backstabber two days ago when we had tea in this kitchen!" Click, click. "I can't believe you didn't mention it once."

Damien stepped between them, since Miranda looked too dazed by the flash to take action.

"Violet, this might not be the best time."

# 8

"VIOLET." I RECOVERED MYSELF enough to close my mouth so I didn't look like a dying fish in all the photographs. "Can we talk privately?"

I hoped I could reason with her somehow, because I sure as heck didn't want her to post those pictures online. Or anywhere.

"Of course." She smoothed her camel-colored, pleated skirt and smiled at Joelle, Damien and Scotty, all of whom had ended up in the living area to witness the drama. "It was the dark hair that threw me off, by the way." Violet pointed to my messy curls, sprouting like demon horns in all directions from my head. "The color is great, but I didn't recognize you when we met. I kept thinking you seemed familiar, though."

She peered down at her camera and pushed some buttons, probably reviewing how ridiculous I looked in Damien's bathrobe with my mouth gaping.

"I was going to take off, anyway," Joelle assured me. "I'm getting a room at a hotel nearby and I can stop back tomorrow. Maybe we can make a date to tour some other properties and see if we can find you a tearoom to get you settled."

My friend already had her sweater over her arm.

"I'll text you and we'll make a plan," I offered, grateful for the help. I really did want to talk to her more. "Thanks for checking on me."

She gave me a hug and a quick kiss on my cheek. "You knew I would."

Soon, Joelle was gone and Damien had disappeared into the kitchen with Scotty. I knew he probably had some animals to check on, anyhow. I wondered when I'd get to be with him alone again. I could hardly believe what had happened between us last night. I'd taken a monumental step with him, even if he didn't know the full extent of what a big deal it had been for me. My old insecurities were already jittering around a little bit inside me, making me wonder how important the night had been to *him*.

I hoped I wasn't the only one still reeling from the realization that we had a powerful connection. What if I was attaching too much meaning to how great the sex had been?

"So...Violet." I waved her over to one of the chunky leather ottomans near the fireplace in the front room. "Have a seat."

"Actually, I'd love to take you to lunch if you have time." She fiddled with the strap on her camera as she perched on the edge of the ottoman. "I'm visiting some local friends this week and they are big fans of the show."

My stomach knotted.

"That's just the thing." I tightened the belt on Damien's robe, wishing I was back in his bed and this day could start all over again. "I'm trying to put the show behind me."

"Why?" she blurted, her delicate, pale features scrunching into a worried frown. "You should be proud! You did a great job and you didn't compromise your values. It doesn't matter about the dopey nickname they gave you, right?"

She spoke with such vehemence, I actually *did* feel a little proud of myself. Not compromising had been important, after all.

"Thank you. I appreciate that. I really do." I reached to give her arm a squeeze, an impulsive gesture she returned. "The problem is, I'd like to keep my whereabouts out of the media, and if my picture is posted with any details about me being in Sonoma County—"

"Oh, no." Violet straightened.

"What?"

"I may have inadvertently—" She bit her lip. "That is—" She pulled a phone from the pocket of her cream-colored blazer. "I think I mentioned…"

"What?" My shoulders tensed. Hot prickles broke out on my skin. What had she done?

Scrolling through brightly colored screens, she slowed down to read a message or text or something.

"I did post a note last night about meeting you. I thought I might have sent it as a private message on Twitter, but it's on my public feed." She flipped her phone around so I could see the screen, but the little box with her note didn't mean that much to me, since I didn't use the program.

The blurb read: Met THE Gutsy Girl, the Nebraska NICE girl, Miranda Cortland, in wine country this weekend. #awesome

"But the note is only seen by your friends, right?" I had a vague understanding of Twitter. Maybe.

"Actually, I have a lot of followers because of my wine blog." Her shoulders slumped as she flipped to another screen. "This message has already been re-tweeted like...seventy-five times."

I tried to process that. "Seventy-five people saw it?"

"No." She pointed to a box that said "Followers." "Ten thousand people follow me. My blog has really grown over the past year."

I felt faint.

"And although I didn't mention Fraser Farm in the tweet about you, there are references to this place in my other posts about our hunt for a racehorse and the visit to a local winery." She kept scrolling for another moment and then set the phone aside. "I'm really sorry, Miranda. It never occurred to me you wouldn't want anyone to know you're here. Not many people go into reality TV to be anonymous."

"It's okay." I said it automatically, my hand going to my dark hair. The dye job had been a waste.

My future here had ended after a few short days. The knowledge rattled around inside me.

*Damien.*

"I hope it won't create any trouble for you?" Violet

sounded genuinely concerned, and she probably was. But apparently, the damage had already been done.

An oil painting of an old Derby winner hanging on Damien's wall went out of focus as I began to feel a little faint. If Rick Barrow was looking for me, he was a Google search away from finding me. As were any psycho fans, star-watchers or TMZ reporters.

The only person who was going to be more disappointed than me? The gorgeous, sexy star of my book and my fantasies. The one man I hadn't wanted to let down.

Damien.

"YOU'RE SURE YOU KNOW how to ride?" Damien asked me the question for at least the third time later that afternoon.

For now, I stroked the older mare's nose while I held the bridle beneath her muzzle. I'd borrowed boots from the tack room that were too big for me, so it was just as well I had a more low-key mount even if I'd always been steady in a saddle. Just because I could ride farm horses at seventeen didn't mean I'd be able to handle a Thoroughbred six years later. But Windchime didn't seem as if she was going to give me any trouble, and I was glad to be away from Violet Whiteman, nice as she might be. She'd promised to look into damage control, and wished me luck in ducking the paparazzi who might make the trek to this part of the state.

I still hadn't told Damien the secret was out about me being here. Call me a coward. I just didn't want to ruin what was left of our time together. I knew as soon as the world came looking for me, I'd need to leave Fraser Farm. He didn't deserve the brand of crazy I'd be bringing to his door. I'd tell him during the ride, though. Definitely.

My stomach cramped. Why had I thought I might find happiness here? I felt I'd been running for six years and finally found a place where I'd be safe.

"I'm positive. I love to ride and I've missed it." I enjoyed his protectiveness. His thoughtfulness.

I watched him check the cinch on his horse, Eclipse, a younger gelding that he'd brought into the Thoroughbred rescue program. Damien really lived the idea of "second chances." He'd sure given me one.

But I couldn't think about that and how much leaving was going to hurt. It was cooler out today and I was glad for the oversize canvas coat I'd snagged from a hook in the barn, even if I looked like a street orphan.

"Ready?" He turned to me, his flannel shirt layered over a blue thermal one, the sleeves rolled up so I could see the muscles flex in his forearms as he rechecked my horse for me.

"Very." Mostly, I was ready to be close to him again. Even though we'd been out of bed for only five hours, I missed the feel of his hands on me. Being with him had been...*spectacular.* That really wasn't too strong of a word for the way he'd made me feel. So unfair that all those good feelings were already tinged with the bittersweet knowledge that they wouldn't last.

"Did I catch a hint of a smile?" He ran a thumb beneath my jaw as he tipped up my face and studied me.

Swallowing hard, I tucked away worries about the

future and savored the now as I buckled the clasp on my helmet.

"I've been thinking about that moment when Wind-chime and I leave you in the dust."

"Is that right?" He hovered closer, his hands going around my waist beneath the big jacket I wore.

I got shivers, but they weren't from the weather.

"Maybe I was also thinking about how good you look in jeans."

"Are you going to write about it?" he teased, his breath warm on my cheek before he kissed my temple.

I felt melty inside already. Maybe I needed to make up for all the years I'd missed out on sex, because I had the urge to drag him back to the house and have my way with him. A switch had been flipped inside me and now that it was turned on, carnal thoughts were never far from my mind.

This wasn't just a sexual awakening for me. It was a sexual thunderbolt.

"Keep inspiring me, hot stuff, and I think I might." I arched up on my toes to kiss him, brushing my lips over his.

The soft, subtle pressure of his mouth reminded me of all the things he'd done to me the night before, the way his kiss had driven me to the edge and back. I inhaled the clean, musky scent of horse and man, my fingers curling into his soft shirt.

His breathing changed, becoming faster, harder, his awareness of me immediately obvious. Arousing. Besides, my pocket of time at Fraser Farm was quickly running out. I needed to act fast to store up more memories before I moved on.

When he pulled back, I barely had a second to meet his fiery gaze before he lifted me by the waist and plunked me into the saddle. Windchime hardly even twitched.

"That's more than enough inspiration for now," Damien growled, the warning in his voice making my toes curl inside the too-big boots I wore.

I didn't bother trying to hide a smile as he stalked over to his horse and flung himself stiffly onto Eclipse's back. Truly happy moments like this one didn't come around nearly often enough.

"Ready?" he asked, taking up his reins and turning the dark gelding around.

We were taking one of the trails he kept groomed so guests could ride the horses they boarded at the farm, or potential buyers could watch a prospective horse's workout.

"I'm ready." My heart still thundered, anticipation for this man warming my blood.

"She won't follow me. She'll wait for you to give her full rein before she'll let loose."

"Got it." I tensed and Windchime shifted. I patted her neck to reassure her I was no nervous horsewoman. Forcing myself to relax, I watched as Damien urged his mount forward.

I waited. And waited. True to Damien's word, Windchime let me call the shots. And once I knew that I could, I leaned forward over her neck, bracing myself even as I loosened her lead and gave the command.

She took off with gratifying speed, her age and calm demeanor not taking away from the fact that this was a Thoroughbred, a horse bred and raised for racing. Her legs worked hard, churning fast and spitting bits of gravel as she got under way.

But after that initial surge, the big bay mare cruised into a smooth gallop that would have left any other horse I'd ever ridden in the dust. I stayed low over the withers, loving the aerodynamic feel of cutting though the cool breeze, the warm animal beneath me. Her pace seemed so effortless, her stride so long and easy that I laughed out loud at the simple joy of it. No one would ever drive an SUV to work if they could ride one of these gorgeous animals instead. My worries about Violet and my whereabouts coming to light rolled off my shoulders.

With wind whipping through the hair that escaped my riding helmet, I crowed long and loud. I might have beaten my chest with my fist if I didn't think it'd make me fall out of the saddle. Damien must have heard me whooping with the fun of it because he turned to look over his shoulder. A wide grin spread across his features when he saw me.

No doubt I was smiling like a fiend, probably catching bugs in the shiny white grille of my teeth.

He slowed his pace just a little and so did I. Steering the shiny black gelding off the packed-dirt trail, he led me into a grassy field, a pasture to my mind. On a horse farm, maybe it had another name. But this was no formal paddock with reinforced split rail fences and partial stone gates. It was a meadow of tall grass and wildflowers, surrounded by old trees. If this part of the land was fenced, I couldn't see any evidence. Maybe we were simply riding the Sonoma County hilltops between Damien's property and the olive grove.

When he slowed down a bit more, I brought Windchime up beside his horse, finally straightening fully for the first time.

"What do you think?" he asked, spreading one arm wide to take in the sweeping view of hills and groves that rolled down to the Pacific in the distance.

"Incredible." I laughed, still giddy from the ride, the man, the afternoon.

But as we stood there, the horses breathing a little harder while they stamped and snorted, my heart expanding with stronger feelings than Damien would ever guess, I knew I had to tell him the truth. He deserved to know that my secret was out. Fraser Farm might already be a destination on the Hollywood map of the stars, Reality TV Edition. Yes, there was such a thing.

Yet the bigger risk came from Rick. He'd never liked it that I took off after he got engaged to Nina. I think he'd envisioned himself having both of the Cortland girls twined around his finger. I had the vague sense he'd try to do something to hurt me, or retaliate against an old perceived slight in some way.

"Miranda?" Damien waved his hand in front of my face, Eclipse nudging Windchime. "It may be a great view, but it sure took you on a journey far, far away from me."

He had no idea how much further apart we were

about to get once I quit running from reality and told him the truth about Violet's visit.

"AND YOU SAW this message Violet said she tweeted?" Damien nudged the gelding around a sharp turn on a path down the far side of one of the hills behind his property. It was a neutral zone here. He'd probably already crossed his property line, but to preserve the natural beauty of the place, he and his olive-growing neighbor kept it free of fences.

He'd planned a special day for Miranda, with the horseback ride and a treat he had waiting for them back at the farm. But the day had taken a slide a hell of a lot steeper than the terrain they navigated now.

"Yes. Not that I understand a lot about Twitter. But she said she had ten thousand followers and her note had already been…I forget what she called it…copied and sent out by seventy-five of them." Miranda's horse shook her head in protest at crossing a small rivulet, but stayed the course.

Damien had quit worrying about Miranda's riding an hour ago, after seeing how well she kept her seat. She had a high comfort level around horses, a fact that Windchime seemed to have grasped early on.

"Re-tweeted," he replied absently, his brain working overtime to think through the implications of what that meant. How much of a following did Miranda have?

The kind that meant photographers might camp out on his property? Or the kind that meant a few fans would troop up to his front door every other week?

"Wow." She gave a dry laugh. "Someone knows his social media terminology."

"I'm a sole proprietor with a fledgling company. I have no choice."

"That's what Joelle says about the tearoom. When you own the company, you do it all. Maybe you can teach—" Miranda stopped abruptly, her jaw snapping shut.

"I'd be happy to share what I know." He looked her way sharply, wondering why she'd cut off the thought. "Why wouldn't I?"

Her shoulders swayed with the motion of the horse, as did the barely there feather earrings that dangled from the delicate silver cuffs on her ear. Her full lips were pursed.

"We both know I won't be sticking around long enough to open that tearoom here, let alone ask for help promoting the business."

He noticed she didn't say anything about the fact that her leaving meant they wouldn't be together. His jaw tightened, but he wasn't ready to tackle that just yet. Hell…they'd only just found each other. Only just crossed that line from strangers to a whole lot more. Why did Violet Whiteman have to show up and rob them of finding out exactly where that might have led?

"We don't know that at all," he said finally. He swung down off his horse and pulled open one of the gates to return them to Fraser Farm property.

"What do you mean?" She urged Windchime through the open gate with nothing more than a shift of her weight, her slender thighs flexing along the mare's back. "Didn't you hear what I just said? The secret is out. My whereabouts have been revealed. All that stuff you didn't want to happen—star-watchers camping on your lawn, tabloid media following you with a camera lens in the hope of a good shot—all that's going to happen now."

"It hasn't happened yet." Taking Eclipse by the reins, he led the gelding into the fenced pasture and closed the gate behind them before he re-mounted. "And who knows when it will? Sonoma is a long drive from Los Angeles."

"Seriously?" She shook her head as if to clear it, the feather earrings dancing just above the collar of her coat. "What happened to your concerns about a reality TV fan base detracting from the upscale ambience you're creating here? You were ready to cart me off the property that first night—"

"And you can't think of any reason I might feel differently about that now?" He wanted her so badly his teeth hurt. That kiss before they began the ride had wound him up.

"Attraction doesn't change a fundamental divide."

"No." But it was more than attraction at work. Simple chemistry didn't explain the way he'd felt when he'd seen her take care of a newborn foal, or when she'd invited Scotty to help himself to food she'd made. "It makes me want to work harder to figure out a way around it, though. What if this mass invasion of Hollywood reality rabble doesn't happen? What if your celebrity status fades next week and we worried about all this for nothing?"

Neither of them mentioned Rick. Damien wasn't sure why she didn't bring him up. But he was already making plans to protect her from that bastard if the guy dared to show his face anywhere near here. There were benefits to being raised the son of Hollywood royalty, and one of them was that he knew a thing or two about personal security. He'd texted his brother Trey for the names of some people he could trust the second it had been obvious to him where Miranda's story was going.

"That'd be surprising but..." She tipped her head into the breeze, breathing deeply. Did the scents of dry grasses and horses remind her of home? "Really, really great."

"So let's not borrow trouble." He could see the barns in the distance and looked forward to the surprise waiting for her at the end of the ride. The temperature had really dipped as the sun sank, and twice he'd seen Miranda run a hand up and down her arm briskly, as if to warm up.

He looked forward to taking on that task himself.

"I would never have guessed you'd take that approach. I had an impression of you as a bit of a cynic." Miranda gently tapped the slack half of the reins against her thigh, the sound of the leather—against her body—making it damn difficult to concentrate.

The need to get her alone—and off the horse—crawled over his skin and heated him from the inside out.

"Then you've got a lot to learn about me, don't you?" He knew he wasn't Joe Friendly. He'd been living like a hermit, trying to get his business off the ground, and the horses didn't require a whole lot of social skills.

But something about Miranda made him want to dust off at least a few of his finer points. And it was more than the fact that the soft tapping of leather against her thigh was driving him wild.

"I'm trying to know you better," she said softly, giving him a sideways glance.

Damn, but he liked seeing her open up to him. Trust him a little bit.

"I've got a surprise for you," he admitted, his voice hoarse with want. No, make that *need.*

"Really?" The tap, tap, tapping of the slack reins on her thigh slowed. Stopped.

He had to swallow hard to keep from dragging her down into the cold grass right here.

"You see that barn on the far right?" They were close enough now to make out several of the stables and barns. Smoke curled from a handful of the stone chimneys. At least one of those fires was wood-burning, the scent a distinct sweetness in the air.

"The one still under construction?" She squinted into the distance, her lips pursing again as she concentrated.

"There's no construction today. I sent the workers over to a different project, to be sure we'd have the place to ourselves."

She raised an eyebrow. "An empty barn?"

"My office is completed. And private." Probably more private than the house, where his friends and her friends dropped by unannounced.

"Oh." Her blue eyes took on a glow that he recognized from other times she'd been focused on him and…excited. A vein throbbed fast in her temple and he wanted to drag his tongue over that spot.

"The surprise is in there." He was so close to being able to do whatever he wanted with her.

"I like surprises." She shifted in the saddle and gave him a slow, steamy appraisal with her eyes. "Race you for it?"

"I think I'd rather watch you as you ride away." The sight of her splayed thighs and subtle curves was a sweet torment he wasn't ready to quit just yet.

"I don't know about that." The heightened color in her cheeks reminded him she wasn't used to such blatant flirting. But when she leaned closer, the soft puff of her breath on his cheek was like a finger stroke across the front of his jeans. "You're probably just afraid you can't keep up."

With a flick of the reins, she took off, her mare responding instantly to a command for speed.

Damien watched her—as promised—her lean body bent low over the animal's back. And while she did look mighty fine from this angle, he hoped like hell he wouldn't be watching Miranda walk away from him any time soon.

# 9

TEARING ACROSS THE FIELDS, I couldn't help but feel just a little bit hopeful. Riding was a thrill I hadn't experienced in so long, and Damien's reaction to my news had been surprisingly…okay. He hadn't gotten surly. Hadn't insisted we turn around and go home to start preparing for the worst.

He still treated me as if he wanted me, and that was a gift I hadn't expected.

I dared a look over my shoulder at one point and saw him coming for me, his horse a dark, charging blur over the green field. Another thrill shot through me and I couldn't believe my luck. He didn't want me to leave. At least not yet.

I didn't mind taking things one day at a time when I didn't know where else to go, anyhow. I would savor every second with Damien. Because even if he couldn't help me forge my dream of running my own business, he had given me something more important. He'd done more to heal my old phobias about men in the past few days than I'd managed in long months of counseling sessions. Even my writing hadn't been as effective as Damien's tenderness and his obvious desire for me.

Last night, I'd actively pushed aside my issues to be with him. By this morning, those issues were still there, but I didn't have to wrestle with them nearly as hard. They stood quietly in the background, nervous but out of my way. It was an amazing feeling.

Ahead of me, I saw Scotty waving one arm by the unfinished barn, and had a moment of worry. What if he was here to tell us that reporters had arrived? That *Gutsy Girl* fans were at the house, waiting for us?

"Hi," I called as I reined in, hoping he could hear me over the music in his headphones. "Everything okay?"

The farmhand tugged aside one earbud. "Just came over for the horses. Damien asked me to bring them in for grooming."

He reached for Windchime's bridle, steadying her.

"Oh." That made sense. This way, we wouldn't have to take care of the animals. I tried not to smile at the apparent planning that had gone into this day. "Thanks."

I slid down on my own, even though Scotty moved to help me. I was in a hurry, eager to see whatever else Damien had in store for us. Now, he trotted to a halt behind me, keeping Eclipse a good distance from Windchime until the feistier horse settled down.

When I glanced his way, Damien was watching me with thinly veiled hunger in his eyes. Was it only me who could see that, or was it obvious to Scotty, too? My cheeks heated even as awareness flickered through me. I busied myself removing my helmet and giving it to

Scotty, while Damien relayed some final instructions about farm business. My own thoughts were a tangle, my emotions clamoring so insistently that I couldn't think straight.

Right now, I was all hunger and instinct. I couldn't keep my eyes off Damien.

"Got it, boss. No problem." Scotty nodded and clamped his headphones back over his ears. He led the horses away from the unfinished barn toward their home stables, closer to the main house.

A young woman jogged toward Damien's assistant. She wore a green field jacket with the Fraser Farm logo. She took one of the horses, neither she nor Scotty looking back. Leaving us alone.

I couldn't think of a thing to say when I met Damien's hazel eyes. Maybe he felt the same, because he stood silently for a long moment, our gazes crawling over each other the way our hands were aching to do. At least, the way mine were.

"Let's go inside." He took my hand, folding it in his. I could feel the warmth of his palm right through my thin leather riding gloves.

We walked into the open space of the central barn, cathedral-like in its current state of half completion. Golden rays from the slowly setting sun angled through the rafters. Wide future stalls were evident from the position of the support columns.

"We'll have some viewing areas for the stallions over here." He pointed out matching open spaces at either end of the barn. "The plumbing was just finished for the washing racks over here. Holding areas for the mares on the opposite end."

I nodded, impressed. "I knew Thoroughbred racing was a big industry, but this is incredible." The facility was mammoth. We walked into the heart of it, the finished section in the center.

Fine stonework covered the walls of what would one day be a receiving area—this one for people, not horses. The floor was dusty from construction, but the bones of the room were obvious. High ceilings, a huge hearth, heavy double doors between rooms all sent a subtle message of old-world elegance.

"I'm working out here now so I can oversee construction on the days when the crew installs important features or needs quick decisions. But one day, within two years, the stallion manager will work in this facility, and I'll move back to the original barns." Damien opened one of the polished wood doors by the wrought-iron handle.

"It looks like the stables from some posh British manor house. A step back in time." The scents of milled wood and some kind of chemical glaze made everything smell brand-new. "I actually looked through a lot of architectural design books when I was thinking up plans for a tearoom."

"A lot about racing is a nod to old traditions." He pointed to some ironwork detailing around built-in bookshelves inside his office. On the shelves were horseshoes in mahogany shadowboxes, and black-and-white photographs of former Triple Crown winners.

But the central feature of the office—at least for

today—was a small café table placed off to one side of the room. It was covered with a white linen cloth, and silver candlesticks held ivory candles that flickered softly in the breeze when the door shut behind us. Two place settings sat alongside covered platters and more silver dishes.

"Wow." I shook my head, unable to reconcile the pickup-driving horse breeder—the dusty guy who'd been surly to me that first day—with the man watching me patiently now. "This is beautiful."

"I thought you deserved a meal prepared for you, instead of cooking for my staff and guests." He shrugged out of his coat and laid it on a polished wood bench near the door. "There's a bathroom in the back if you'd like to wash up."

A tingling started in my chest. I couldn't think of it as warm fuzzies, since that sounded like something a six-year-old felt for her teddy bear, and what I felt about Damien right now was a whole lot more grown-up. But there was a definite tenderness growing in the region of my heart.

"That would be great." I realized how overenthusiastic I sounded about an offer to use a restroom. Weird how that awkward teenager I'd once been still emerged at the oddest times. "I mean…thanks."

I ducked in the other direction to wash the grit of horse and leather from my hands and face. Toweling off on the thick white terry cloth that hung on a brand-new pewter dowel, I had a stern stare-down with myself in the mirror.

*Don't read too much into this. Don't get all mushy romantic inside because a guy treats you to dinner.*

How pathetic would I be if I fell over the first guy to do something so sweet? The fact that I'd pushed men away with both hands for years was the only reason I was such a relationship newbie. The only reason Damien's careful plans for a date today had me dreaming about a romantic future.

*Relax.*

When I came out of the bathroom, Damien was just returning to the office from somewhere else in the half-finished building, a towel around his neck. His short hair was damp and pushed back from his face. His shirt a little more open at the collar than it had been.

My heart rate quickened. My breath caught. I stared at him, frozen, while he shut the door quietly. Locked it.

He caught my stare. Must have seen the way I eyed him like a drink after a hike through the desert.

"Hungry?" His gaze never left mine. I swear those hazel eyes pulled me to him as if I was on a string.

"Starving," I whispered, right before I pressed myself against him, pressed my lips to his.

He didn't seem to mind. In fact, the few noises he made while I kissed the ever-loving daylights out of the man sounded full of approval.

Eyes closed, arms twined around his neck, I backed him against the heavy wooden door. Kissing, wanting, panting. I peeled one layer of shirt off and then the other, until his chest was hot and naked against mine, the sculpted lines of smooth abs and narrow waist almost as appealing as the flat surface of his pectorals or the broad expanse of shoulders.

Looking wasn't enough, though. I smoothed my hands over the warm, hard planes and drew deep, wet kisses from him until we were both edgy and excited.

"I'm in charge," I warned him between kisses, savoring the way he let me do as I pleased.

"I'm strangely in the mood for taking orders." His hands roamed over my body with all the self-assurance of a guy who knew exactly what he was about.

"No." I gripped his wrists in manacles of thumbs and forefingers, not reaching all the way around. "I mean—I'm in charge."

*Shaelynn speaks!* The notion flashed through my head, the idea of a character speaking through me not nearly as absurd as it should have been. I needed her strength. Her confidence. If I didn't have much time left with Damien, I needed every second to count, every encounter to push me further toward becoming a normal, sensual, sexually empowered woman.

I felt his smile in a stretch of his lips beneath mine, a sensation that seemed sexy on the outside even as it warmed my heart. *Yes!*

"Can't wait to see what you're going to do with me," he teased, his wrists going slack in my hands, the muscles in his forearms relaxing.

The action between his hips and mine…that didn't relax one bit. Quite the opposite.

Bolstered, I rocked against him, liking the hard feel of him and the knowledge that I'd done it to him. I raised his arms higher, to shoulder height. Higher still.

"Am I your prisoner?" he asked, an eyebrow quirked as I kept going.

"Mostly I just like seeing things flex." I dipped down to kiss his shoulder, where muscles had popped into delicious relief. Then I bent lower, to lick a kiss along the top of his biceps. "You taste good."

I nipped a soft bite there, but he flexed again, making it impossible to get a hold on him. I kept him pinned in place, looking, and liking what I saw. Until I glanced into his eyes and saw a starker hunger there.

"What?" I loosened my hold.

"It's nothing." He shook his head. Stayed right where I'd left him, even though I wasn't really holding him anymore.

Confused, I rubbed a finger against his arm. More friendly, less sexy. "Did I mess something up?"

Doubts crowded my mind, a quick avalanche of negative thoughts—

"No." He grabbed me by the shoulders—gently. "Look at me. You could never mess this up. Ever. I'm so turned on I can't think straight, which is why I…" He shook his head as if to clear it. "You said that thing, you know—'you taste good.'"

"I remember." I was holding the avalanche at bay. Or he was. I liked the way he held me. Talked to me.

I definitely liked how he looked at me. There was a sincerity in this man's gaze that I was certain never left. He could be cynical. Unsocial, even. But he was honest. He didn't have that layer of charm that most of Hollywood wore like a second skin. I'd bet anything he'd shed it like a hot potato when he moved up here.

"My brain went to all kinds of carnal places on that one." He shook his head again, but this time, it seemed to be a gesture of regret. "I tried to rein in my imagination in the same way I held still for you, but I guess some of what I was thinking registered in my face."

"Oh." I tried to put that together. I'd said he tasted good. In turn, he'd thought… *"Oh."*

I got it now. His expression hadn't been disappointed. Or frustrated because I didn't know what I was doing, or because I wasn't my sister. He just wanted more. Of me.

He wanted really sexy things from me.

"Yeah. Oh." He cleared his throat. "And that was just a stray, crazy, hot thing I was thinking about you, because I could think hot things about you 24/7 and still wake up wanting more."

"Okay." I nodded, more wild about this man than ever. What kind of magic did he possess to banish that whole storm of negative thoughts that had been about to slam over me? "Things are getting interesting, aren't they? I like hearing that…you know…you want me."

I pulled off my sweater in a move that had Damien's undivided attention. It stuck on my forehead a little, but he helped tug it off and over, his attention…fixed. Heated. I didn't even think about my body or bother to be self-conscious.

I was back in the Sexy Zone.

"Will you come lie down?" I asked, taking his hand.

There was a monstrous leather sectional at the far end of the room that looked like it could accommodate six grown men without them touching, so I figured it would work for us.

Dusk was falling fast outside, the purple light filtering in and making the candlelight seem brighter as I led him toward the corner.

"Want me to undress?" he asked hopefully, as he took a seat on the couch, the brick-red leather softly squeaking.

"I'm doing all the undressing here." Just this once, I needed to be in charge. I hadn't realized it until I started this little game of sexual dictatorship, but I was loving the power trip. Loving that he indulged me. "First I go. Then I'll do you."

He groaned as if this would be a unique brand of torment, but I was too busy unclasping my bra to pay attention. I wasn't smooth about it, but somehow I unhooked the back with fingers that trembled. Slowly, I edged the straps off my shoulders, my touch lingering over smooth skin, senses ultra-aware. Shivers raced up my arms, my nails lightly grazing the sensitive back of one and then the other as I unwound myself from lace and satin.

Breasts beading even though the room was warm, I made a halfhearted attempt to cover myself. Not that I was embarrassed about my body—I'd conquered those old evils long ago. But I wanted his attention on what was going to be unveiled next.

Instead, his gaze snapped up to mine.

"Thank you." The fierceness in his voice made me wonder how I'd earned the gratitude. Now, of all times.

"For what?" My fingers paused over the button of my jeans.

"I wanted to do something nice for you today, and

instead, you're giving me…" His eyes burned me like a candle flame. "…something so much better."

My heart turned over in my chest.

"You're an easy man to please." I cupped his face, savoring the warmth of his jaw, the rough feel of five o'clock shadow.

I didn't want to ever leave this place. Not Fraser Farm. Not this office. Not this moment. Even the thrill of sexual dominance didn't compare with the soul-deep connection I felt to this man right now.

DAMIEN FELL FOR HER.

Hard.

He could feel himself going over the edge, and couldn't do a thing to stop it even though he knew Miranda Cortland could vanish out of his life as quickly as she'd charged into it. She was so damn vivid, so bright, so too-good-to-be-true, he half wondered if he'd dreamed her.

"Is it my turn yet?" he asked, needing to break the spell, needing to just get his hands on her so he could channel all of what he was feeling into making her feel good. "To touch you?"

He took a risk and cupped her bare waist, the skin creamy and soft. High, perfect breasts turned up at the tips, just out of reach of his mouth. When she didn't protest, he kissed just beneath the left one and caught the barest hint of fragrance. Something warm and sweet, like vanilla.

"You can have a turn," she agreed, her hands stroking his arms and shoulders, the grazing touch winding him up again. "I'll reserve the rights to a full striptease another day."

"I'm going to hold you to that." He wanted to squeeze her tighter. Make sure she stayed. "I may need to work up the stamina to withstand it."

"Was it so painful?"

"Seeing you get naked and not touch you?" He looked up at her in the flickering candlelight, her skin tinged with warm, golden tones. "I wouldn't call it painful so much as…a test of restraint."

He spanned her rib cage with one hand and lowered a kiss to her flat abdomen just above the waistband of her jeans. Just below the belly-button snake ring that had driven him crazy that first day.

"Doesn't anyone ever tell you *no?*" she teased, her hands combing through his hair, down the back of his neck, over his shoulders.

"Not anyone that I've ever wanted to say *yes* to this badly." Unfastening the clasp on the denim, he shoved her jeans down her hips, kissing his way along the lace trim of neon pink panties.

She stilled when he dipped his tongue beneath the edge, tasting her soft skin. Her nails flexed into his flesh and she gasped.

Pushing the denim farther down her legs, he coaxed one foot off the ground and then the other, tugging the jeans away and the pink underwear with them.

"Now you," she urged, rotating her finger in a spinning motion, as if to show him how fast she wanted him to move. "Can you take those off?"

He could see the flush in her cheeks and the bright

light in her blue eyes that said she wanted this as much as him. There was no more taking their time. Without answering, he stood to wrestle worn jeans over unyielding flesh, kicking aside boxer shorts, too. The only thing he kept was the condom packet he placed on an arm of the sofa. But before he could lower her onto the couch with him, she sank to her knees in front of him.

And he'd thought he was done testing his restraint? He bit the inside of his cheek as she brushed soft lips up the rigid length of his shaft. The sight of her kissing and tasting him, her hands splayed on his hip bones, sent a hot surge through his blood. Grinding his teeth together, he tried not to think about how good she felt or how sweet she looked or how much he wanted to be inside her before he lost it.

But he waited. Held back. Twined his fingers in wild curls that would be gorgeous any color she dyed them. And only when his release was imminent—tingling in the base of his erection and driving him out of his ever-loving mind—did he lift her to her feet. Her satisfied smile made his restraint worth it, that sweet, feminine confidence obvious.

He didn't let her savor the moment, though. He'd waited until the last possible second, and now he needed her. Tearing apart the condom packet he'd left out, he rolled on protection. Lowered her to the wide leather cushions of the sectional and positioned himself between her thighs.

Light freckles sprinkled across her chest and shoulders called to his tongue. He kissed a path between them, licking and nipping his way across her collarbone while he coaxed a finger inside her. Tested her warmth and heat. She arched her back. Rolled her hips into his touch.

He could have touched her like that all day if he hadn't already been pushed to the edge himself. But she was more than ready for this. For him. The slick wetness on his finger drove him wild. He circled her sex, rolling his thumb along the swollen nub, working the sensitized flesh until she moaned and undulated against him.

When he entered her, she tossed her head back, urging him on with sweet, incoherent words of encouragement. She wanted him, she needed him, please, please, please....

Like a siren's call, the breathy sound of her made him forget everything except this moment. Except eliciting the next soft moan for more. He thrust his hips harder. Faster. She moved with him until her legs locked around his waist, holding him fast. She arched hard against him, hips grinding into his as she found her release.

Feminine muscles tightened and contracted, softened and then tightened again. And again. Miranda was caught in a storm of sweet, sensual waves, her whole body riding the crest of that hot momentum. He held her through it, taking all those lush, intimate touches until her hips stopped bucking, her thighs loosening just a little.

Then he thrust just twice more. Burying himself deep inside her, he came so hard he saw stars. *Stars.* That wasn't waxing poetic. He was pretty sure it was the return of oxygen and blood to his brain, after his body had held it hostage for so long to fuel the headiest sex of his life.

Collapsing to one side so as not to crush her, he waited for his breath to return. Or his senses. He could have slept with her in his arms right there all night and been perfectly content.

But this date wasn't supposed to be about him. He'd arranged the horseback ride for her. A meal they hadn't eaten—for her. He needed to stop getting distracted with how much he wanted her, and focus on how he could keep her.

"Miranda?" He couldn't move yet, but he was speaking. It was a start.

"Hmm?"

He smiled a little, to think coherent speech was a struggle for her, too.

"Are you hungry?"

# 10

"Mmm." The appreciative rumble in the back of Damien's throat let me know he was enjoying the game we played an hour later as we half sat, half sprawled near each other on the office floor. "That tastes so good."

A shiver of pleasure went through me as I understood why those same words, when I'd spoken them earlier tonight, had made him think sexy thoughts. They did the same for me now. I fanned myself.

Not that Damien could see, since he was blindfolded.

"But what does it taste *like?*" I prompted, sitting cross-legged on the floor in front of him, the remains of our picnic scattered around. We'd eaten everything in a nest of blankets spread over the Persian carpet, like a couple of decadent Roman nobles.

I leaned back against the displaced leather couch cushion and waited for his verdict. I'd used the office's coffeepot to heat water for tea, since I always carried a small stash in my purse. Tea bags take up about as much room as an extra tissue, and that way I always have my favorite flavors. So after a lunch catered by a local winery, I'd come up with the idea of a taste test.

"It reminds me of you." He lifted the edge of his shirt up over one eye to look at me, the rest of the flannel still tied around his head, where I'd secured it earlier. His chest was, happily, naked. He'd pulled on his jeans for dinner and I'd worn his other shirt.

"Me?" I laughed, a little giddy from my one glass of wine. Plus I'd thrown myself into the "live for the moment" idea and wanted to squeeze every second of joy that I could out of this window of time with Damien. "I'm pretty sure I don't taste anything like tea."

"I definitely recall a hint of vanilla." He set down the cup I'd given him and shoved the flannel blindfold the rest of the way off. "Right here." He leaned over a crimson chenille throw blanket and brushed his fingertips along the spot just beneath my breast through the fabric of the cotton shirt I wore. "I kissed you there and the scent of you reminds me of this tea. Vanilla."

My breasts felt heavy with awareness, the nipples beading as soon as he touched me. Since I hadn't bothered to put my bra back on, I knew he could tell, now that the blindfold lay forgotten on the floor.

"Well." I tried to ignore the pheromones back at work between us. My eyes went to his lips as I thought about him kissing me there. "You have an excellent sense of taste, it seems. That one is vanilla with cinnamon."

His smile was part triumph and part pure wickedness.

"Are you sure? Because I can put my mouth on you

again and double-check." He was already coming for me across the blanket, the discarded silver trays and lids clanking as he disturbed them.

"I have a better way of testing it." I skittered backward, laughing. "There's another tea you haven't tried."

He sat down, planting an arm on the leather ottoman that had been his backrest a moment ago. "Seriously?" He frowned while I poured hot water over the bag in yet another disposable cup. "How much tea does one woman need on a horseback ride?"

"It's just a little tin." I held it up to show him a case no bigger than most women's compacts, the fabric of my T-shirt dragging across my taut, sensitive left nipple. "I keep a handful of tea choices in there so I have them with me most any time."

"What made you decide you want to run a tearoom?" He took the cup from me, but didn't drink out of it. The scents wafted between us, a complex bouquet he'd probably never guess. "It's a long way from small-town farmer's daughter to Hollywood actress to tearoom proprietor."

"The acting thing was just a stopgap." I knew that even going into it. "I wanted a more exotic life—some reason to feel like I was running *to* something instead of running away from the past. And since lots of people dream of going into show business, I could tell myself it was a step forward, even though I was just sort of… biding time."

"What kinds of jobs did you land? Anything I would have seen?"

"Depends how you feel about late night infomercials for skin cream or advertisements for local fast-food chains."

"That bad?"

"No." I had purposely trotted out the bottom-of-the-barrel jobs to make him smile, but instead his brow wrinkled with worry. "I had tiny roles in a few movies and landed a minor character in a sitcom that didn't get picked up after one season. But it was enough for me to hold my head high when my parents would call and tell me to return home."

Those rare conversations hadn't been a case of my parents trying to welcome me back with open arms. Those talks had been not-so-subtle coercion to admit I'd made a mistake. But that hadn't happened, and it wouldn't happen. I'd protected myself from the past for six years, and I planned to keep on protecting myself from it, even if that meant turning my back on something that might have been really good with Damien. He didn't want more drama in his life, and me? I was the drama queen in more ways than one, even if I didn't want to be.

Damien drank some of the tea I'd made and then inhaled the scent drifting toward him in a tendril of steam, as if still trying to identify the tastes. I liked that he paid careful attention to the game we played. It lifted my spirits as we talked about stuff that I found kind of depressing.

"And when did you start working for Joelle?"

"Almost as soon as I arrived in L.A." I took Damien's half-finished vanilla-cinnamon tea and sipped. "Joelle's place was close to my first apartment, so I could walk there. I'd been on the staff for about a year—hostessing for the restaurant and running the register for the store—when I realized I had much more fun at my part-time job than I did pounding the pavement for acting work."

"What do you like about it?" He polished off his tea and set the cup aside. Candlelight still flickered above us, casting appealing shadows on his face. "The cooking? The customers?"

"I'm good at it." I'd never thought about that before. "All my life, I searched for something that was just mine—something my sister wasn't better at than me. I was always a better cook, but that was never celebrated in my family, because I used the skill to make things like homemade cream puffs and buttery cobbler…all kinds of great treats that made me put on too much weight." Definitely not a healthy coping mechanism for family stress. "But now I can cook for other people and watch them enjoy it."

"I enjoyed the tea," he said suddenly, turning the conversation in a direction I hadn't expected. "But I'm not sure I could tell you anything that was in it."

"Guess your taste buds aren't as refined as I thought."

"Or else I have a taste for you, and only you." He reached across the blanket to palm my bare thigh, his warm, callused hand covering half my leg.

I was a sucker for those calluses. They snagged lightly on the hem of my T-shirt and gently abraded my skin.

"That sounds like a come-on line, if ever I heard one." I walked my fingers up his muscular forearm to his upper arm. His shoulder.

"How's it working?" He came closer again, leaning in to nibble at my neck.

Shivers tripped up and down my spine as I swayed toward him.

"Really, really well." My heart rate spiked wildly, my whole body caught up in the magnetic draw of his. "I wish—"

I stopped myself before I finished that thought.

But not, apparently, before he'd heard me.

"You wish what?" He quit kissing my neck to cup my jaw and stroke his thumb over my cheek.

Putty. I was total putty in his hands. Maybe that's why a little dream of my heart leaped out.

"I wish we had more time."

I knew it was the wrong thing to say even as I said it. Those words changed the mood from lighthearted and fun to brooding and intense. Damien's eyes turned a shade darker, his expression transforming into the hard lines I remembered from that first time we'd met, on the side of the road.

"We can take all the time we want." His voice was serious, the tone full of warning. "You don't need to let anybody chase you away from here if you want to stay."

"I don't feel like I'm being chased." Maybe a little, I did. I'd seen a few overnight sensations in Hollywood wake up to the mayhem of superstardom, only to realize they no longer had a life. "More like this simple existence is about to implode. The quietness of the farm. The fun of new guests. Being part of a new foal's first days…"

"You like the farm more than me." Damien tipped my face up to the candlelight, his expression serious.

"No." I shook my head. "But I think it's great how you built this haven away from everything. You didn't like Hollywood so you got out. And you found a world that suited you much better." I brushed a kiss along his bronzed, rippling shoulder muscle.

Shaelynn would eat her heart out to see me now.

"That's the key, though. I built something. And that means you have to stick around long enough to let a plan develop. To let a dream build."

"I'll do that, too." The words sounded hollow even as I said them. "As soon as I find the right place."

"Then I've got good news for you." Damien's mouth flattened into a hard line.

"Really?"

He didn't look like a man with good news. He looked stoic. Resigned. Determined. And so damn sexy I almost didn't hear what he said next.

"I'm selling you the farm stand."

DAMIEN FIGURED HE'D make it work. Paparazzi on the lawn, star-gazers rubbernecking around his paddocks and a brand of media attention that flew in the face of everything he'd tried to create at Fraser Farm. But this was Miranda, and he couldn't let her go.

"Don't be ridiculous." She gulped down the rest of her tea and set the cup aside, her fingers jittery as she ran them through her hair.

"You've wanted that property since before you even laid eyes on it." She'd drawn that amazing sketch for what the place would look like when she was done, had brainstormed names and even brought some inventory for the store portion of the business, judging by the cases of tea now in his kitchen. "How is it being ridiculous to accept your offer?"

"There's a lot of reasons." She hooked her finger in the collar of her T-shirt and twisted the fabric, a nervous gesture he'd never seen before.

Reaching for her, he untwined the finger and held her hand instead, but he could feel the tension still humming through her.

"Name one." He breathed in the scents in the air, the spices of the tea, the sweetness of Miranda. Would she answer him or would they avoid the topic by getting naked again?

"You don't want the kind of negative press I'll bring."

His gut tightened, and as much as they needed to figure this out, he half wished they could just go back to touching each other. Forgetting everything else but how much pleasure they gave one another.

"I've decided I'm tougher than I gave myself credit for on that score."

"You can't afford to lose business because of me."

"Maybe we can link the *Gutsy Girl* win with the growing side of my business that's going to retrain Thoroughbreds. Spin something about the Nebraska Nice Girl's return to her farm roots to help the horses." He'd just made that up on the spot, but it didn't sound half-bad. Miranda did have a natural affinity for animals. And it did take guts to retrain edgy, high-strung

Thoroughbreds, so it wasn't a task for the average horse owner.

"That's…" Her blue eyes went wide as she digested what he'd said. "…clever but crazy. I don't know anything about retraining Thoroughbreds."

"But you'd make a great spokesperson to promote another 'come from behind' winner." He actually really liked the idea. Was it because of her influence that he was thinking outside the box? "I'm going to need to separate the brand identities for the breeding business and the Thoroughbred rehab business soon, anyhow."

She bit her lip. He could feel her holding back. A deep unease stirred inside him. He'd expected her to go slow in a relationship. Knew she'd had problems in the past and that she had a tendency to run. But he'd thought the property for her tearoom would be his ace…a surefire means of keeping her close.

He didn't invite people into his world often. Hell, he'd made an effort to keep people *out* after the invasiveness of the press in his teenage years. Now that he wanted to share this world he'd created with someone, he didn't know how to make it happen.

"I wanted you to sell that property to me, but I can't let you do it as a favor. That doesn't feel right to me."

"It's not a favor." He was certain of that much. He wanted to keep her safe, damn it. That motive was his alone.

"But a few days ago you thought it didn't make good business sense." She shook her head, frowning. "I can't take the deal just because we started a relationship. That will only lead to trouble and resentment down the road if things don't work out for us."

How could she be slipping away from him already? She'd just landed in his life, made herself important and knocked a crack in his heart before he knew what hit him. Now she was already talking about things not working out?

"You make it sound like leaving is inevitable." He had to be misunderstanding her. This was just beginning, not ending. "What happened to wait and see? Not borrowing trouble? Enjoying the freaking moment?"

"I'm still looking at properties in the area." She fidgeted with the braided corner of a throw pillow, and the sticker on her fingernail made him want to kiss her and forget about any talk of her leaving. "I might find something close by."

"So now I have to talk you into buying the place?" He scraped a hand through his hair, frustrated.

Before she could answer, a scuffling noise sounded outside the closest window.

"Did you hear something?" Miranda asked, going still beside him.

He put his finger to his lips, listening for any other sounds. Tension threaded through him, pulled tight. Was that voices outside?

*"Over there,"* she mouthed, pointing to the window to his left.

He hadn't pulled the blinds, since they were almost 20 acres from the main house and the center of the farm. But as he glanced in the direction she pointed, a bright light flashed against the glass. A shout sounded.

"Ohmigod." Miranda clutched his arm and scrambled behind the desk. "Tabloid media."

He'd been out of the Hollywood circus for so long he almost couldn't compute that. Photographers? On a construction site in the middle of his property?

A quick succession of flashes followed and raised voices could be heard.

"She's here!" someone shouted outside the glass, while Miranda clutched at Damien's wrist and dragged him behind the desk.

"Miranda!" voices called, and a knock sounded on the office door. "Miranda!"

Her face went white as a sheet, and soon a flash went off at another window on the opposite side of the office, while the two of them sat amid still-warm blankets, the candelabra flickering on the table nearby. They were surrounded and under siege by reality TV fans.

Their time alone together had ended way too soon.

# 11

"How are we going to get out of here?" I tried not to panic, but I hated that this crap had followed me so far from Los Angeles. Hated that Damien had to deal with it now.

I should have never bought into the whole "wait and see" approach. I should have bailed the moment I knew Violet Whiteman had broadcast the news of my whereabouts far and wide.

"I've got a plan." Damien stood and went to the closest window. He lowered the wooden blinds and pulled the heavy taupe tapestry drapes closed, ignoring the flashes going off in his face.

He repeated the same deliberate action at three other windows, sealing us in privacy again. But it wasn't the same being alone with him now that we could hear the hubbub of entertainment reporters and photographers just outside, looking for a quick buck. Damien blew out two of the candles, so only one burned in the candelabra.

Now we stared at one another in the dim light, the remains of our fun afternoon scattered all around us like the debris of a tornado. Empty teacups, wineglasses, luncheon plates... I wished we could go back to those moments after we'd touched each other on the couch.

"I'll get Scotty over here." Damien already had his cell phone out and his shirt back on. He tossed me my jeans. "He can distract the reporters. Threaten police action. We'll have someone else—whoever is around the barns tonight—pull around back with my truck and make a break for it."

Before I could comment on the plan one way or another, he was pacing around the office and barking orders into the cell. His expression seemed tense, dark brows drawn together and jaw flexing.

I'd done that to him. I'd stolen his peaceful haven—the retreat from the Hollywood world he'd put behind him—and brought trouble to his door.

"We'll have reinforcements soon," he told me as he disconnected the call and pocketed the phone. "And we've got a good exit strategy. Don't worry."

He put his arms out for me and I stepped into them before I could think about whether that was right or wrong. Just now I needed to feel his strength against me.

"Sounds like you've planned a few exit strategies before," I mumbled into his shirt, planting a kiss above his heart, where I wish I belonged.

"My parents attracted big drama wherever they went, so if I didn't want to be a part of it, I needed to be good at finding back doors, bathroom windows or exits through the kitchen." He kissed the top of my head while the world seemed to fall apart outside in a muted roar of voices. I saw a big white flash under the door. Damien pointed to it. "They're setting up their fill lighting to make sure they get a good shot when we come out. No shadows in the shot equals more money."

"Why did you dislike that life so much?" I asked, seized with the need to discover more about him even though I knew our time together was coming to a close. I had to make tracks to keep reporters away from the farm, to ensure they didn't mess up Damien's careful plans for the future.

"A lot of reasons." He cleared a space on the edge of the cherry desk and we sat there, side by side.

"Tell me some." I tipped my head onto his shoulder, hoping he wouldn't become surly and retreat now. Not yet. Not with me.

"My parents' work didn't involve me, so I don't know why my every move had to be photographed. As a teen-ager, I had my first date chronicled in *Teenplus Magazine.* Right down to where I dropped the girl's ice cream cone."

"Ugh." I could only imagine.

"Yeah, right. A laugh-fest to the rest of the world, but it was definitely not funny to a fifteen-year-old. Then, the girls started a competition to be my prom date. Not because they cared about being with me. They just wanted the magazine spread that came with being a Fraser son's date."

His muscles tensed, his jaw tightening. No matter how lightly he related the story, it was obvious the in-cident had bothered him. Deeply.

"It must be difficult not knowing if someone wants to be with you for your own sake or because of who you know."

Damien snapped his fingers. "That's it. In a nutshell. Tinsel Town B.S. You never knew who your real friends were."

My chest squeezed tight for him. No wonder he'd thrived here with the farm owner, someone who'd helped him realize his potential. Plus the horses...

"That's why you like the farm." I nodded. "Animals are unbiased. They don't judge. And I think they make much better decisions about who to trust than we do."

I remembered how much time I'd spent in the barns as a kid. The dogs, the horses and the chickens all preferred me over Nina. Actually, the cows would have, too, but Nina never got close enough to let the bovine population make that distinction.

"I never thought about it like that, but...I guess." His body language remained tense. "Maybe that is a bonus."

His phone chimed. He picked it up with a speed that told me how ready he was to get out of this conversation. Turning on the screen, he read a message.

"Scotty's pulling up in a minute. We need to be set to run, okay?" He pushed off the desk and moved to the window, carefully lifting the wooden blind enough to see outside. "Are you ready?"

I'd never be ready.

Because leaving this office put me one step closer to leaving Fraser Farm. And Damien.

"We're going through that window." He pointed toward one on the opposite wall from the door. "Run dead ahead and don't look back. There will be a pickup truck with the lights off."

"You're coming with me, right?" I felt nervous as he double-checked his phone and peered carefully out the slit between the blinds again.

"I'm going to run interference." He looked so stern. This was his surly side, the one I'd met that first day. "I'll join Scotty out front to make sure these people need to know they're treading on shaky ground being here. As the property owner, I can stall them longer than Scotty can."

"I'm on my own." I swallowed hard, hating the idea of running across the cold, dark grounds on my own. Knowing that this was goodbye.

"Don't be ridiculous. The driver will take you back to the house. He has instructions to stick with you every second. Just wait for me there and we'll figure out what to do next."

I nodded, but I didn't meet his gaze.

"Don't leave until I get there." He took me by the shoulders, probably guessing my plan. "You have to wait until we can talk about this."

"We *have* talked about it." I spoke softly now that we had the window open. I didn't want any paparazzi to overhear us. "I'm not going to throw you back into the spotlight. I won't do that to you, and I won't do that to your business."

I wanted Fraser Farm to be a success, and I knew you didn't build a Thoroughbred dynasty with a reality TV actress as the face of your brand. My tacky, scandal-ridden image would be a blight on all his hard work.

His hands fell away from me and I felt the chill all the way to my toes.

"You can't run every time things get tough." His voice sounded cool, remote.

I felt my defenses rising fast, shielding me from the hurt I knew was coming, a hurt that no physical boundaries or distance were going to fix.

"This isn't about me, Damien, and this isn't about things getting difficult for *me*." I'd lived through bad times. Fought through them. Emerged stronger.

I thought about my hard-won self-esteem, and the book I was writing, and all the ways I'd worked to heal myself.

"Then if you're doing this for me, I'm telling you flat out—I don't want you to go."

I knew he believed that now. But over time, he would grow to resent me and all the notoriety I'd bring to his life. He'd be too honorable to say anything, but that tension would always be there, and I'd always regret it if I did that to him.

"I can't do that to you. And I won't do that to us." It took all my strength to say it, but I wasn't going to be selfish. I cared about Damien too much. I'd seen what fame had done to Joelle's business, and she was my best friend. How could I put that burden on the shoulders of a guy who'd left his own family to escape life in the glass house that tabloid media could put you in?

"This isn't your call to make, Miranda." He reached for me. Squeezed my forearm. "Rick could be out there looking for you. You need protection, especially now that the news has spread that you're here."

"Rick has known where I lived for the last six years. Just because I don't want to ever see the bastard's face again doesn't mean he's going to hurt me." I wasn't going to let Rick run my life, especially not based on a bogus phone message from a sister who'd never liked me. "I'll be careful."

"If you go anywhere, take the driver with you. That's not optional, and I'm texting him now to let him know he needs to stick by you." Damien's cell phone buzzed while he spoke. He didn't check it, but we both knew what it meant.

It was time to make our break for it. If we didn't move now, the throng of photo hounds would catch us in their lenses and we'd be on the late-night edition of every TV and pop entertainment blog imaginable.

Outside, a voice sounded through a bullhorn. Scotty must be rounding up the trespassing vultures to warn them off.

"Fine. The driver can go with me to Joelle's hotel, but that's it." I tucked my hair behind my ears and slung my lightweight purse under my jacket, as I'd worn it while we were riding. "This is exactly the kind of life you ran from once, too, isn't it?" I asked, imagining fifteen-year-old Damien on that first date as I backed closer to the window.

"Damn it, Miranda, we don't need to run from it anymore." He double-checked to be sure the coast was clear and then slid the window open for me, resigned to our quickly patched together plan.

I knew it was easier this way, even if it did hurt like hell.

"Tell me this. If we don't need to run, then why did we set it up so I'd escape out a back window?" I asked, unable to resist, unable to stop hoping for just an instant that he would prove my fears wrong. I hoisted myself up on the sill with a speed and skill acquired from months of dodging the press.

Damien's mouth worked for a second, as if he wanted to find an answer to that one. My heart sank, because we both knew the truth. He didn't want this kind of life any more than I did. And since he had to stay here for the sake of his business, I had to leave.

I wanted to kiss him goodbye. To feel that amazing connection with him one more time. But I was scared that if I did, the connection would be gone. What if I'd just made him realize I'd never been the right woman for him at all? That these few days we'd had together had been a fluke, and he really was better off without me? I didn't want to know what that kind of bittersweet kiss would feel like.

I'd rather remember those kisses when it had all felt magical. Almost as if we were falling in love.

"Thanks for holding the press off as long as you can." As much as I wanted to be with him, it would be easier to escape with Damien out there. "I'll go fast."

Dropping to the ground outside the office, I felt the night dew on the long grass. Without looking back, I ran toward the pickup truck and an uncertain future. Leaving somewhere—someone—had never been hard for me before, but this time, I ran as if I had bricks on my feet. I guess because I'd left my heart behind.

# 12

"FOR A GUY WHO wanted to put the tabloids behind him, you sure got involved with the wrong woman," Damien's older brother, Trey, observed in a video call later that night.

Damien had his laptop open in the kitchen, right where Miranda had sat with her friend that very morning. Amazing how much emptier a room seemed without her in it. He had a hole in his chest the size of a fist, knowing she was gone. He'd warned off most of the reporters out on the construction site and then stuck around to personally escort a few jokers who hadn't understood the message the first time.

When he got back to the house, her few belongings were gone. The only thing she'd left behind? A case of that cinnamon vanilla tea, right on the floor of the kitchen where Joelle had left it for her. Just looking at it made the hole in his chest widen.

At least she'd taken the driver with her. Bill had

texted a few minutes ago to say they were on the way to Joelle's hotel, the Sea Wind.

"I had no choice in that one, brother." Damien scraped a hand through his hair, wondering where Miranda would go in the morning. "She just plowed into my life and made herself...indispensable."

At least Joelle would be with her in case Barrow showed up. Damien was glad he'd gotten the SUV fixed and the broken lock taken care of today.

"I know a thing or two about indispensable women." On the other end of the video call, Trey sat on the patio of his fiancée's Mar Vista house, the turquoise pool glowing with pink floating candles behind him.

It was a change from the stark existence he'd led up until he met Courtney Masterson, his soon-to-be wife, but he seemed happier and more at peace these days. Then again, he'd need to be at peace to go back into business with their father. Damien had no idea how they'd mended that broken fence, but more power to them for figuring it out.

"So you understand that I can't just...let her go, to face this idiot ex-boyfriend of hers who is looking for her." Damien double-checked his most recent text to a friend in the local cop shop. After talking to the police tonight about the slew of camera-wielding trespassers, he'd given his buddy on the force a heads-up about the possibility of Rick Barrow being in the area.

Didn't matter that the guy had never threatened her. The truth was, Miranda didn't want to be anywhere near him, so Damien would do everything in his power to make sure she stayed safe. If he couldn't have her at his side, he would do whatever he could from afar.

"I've got a great security company. They can have a team up there—" Trey checked his watch, a fancy-ass Breitling that was the kind of thing Damien never wore anymore except to meet with possible Thorough-bred buyers " —just before dawn. In fact, I'll shoot my guy a note right now."

Trey was already at work on his cell phone.

"Whatever it costs." Damien wouldn't let photogra-phers or Nina's smarmy ex-husband within fifty feet of Miranda.

"This one is on Pops, Damien." Trey grinned over the video feed. "The old man needs concrete ways to make it up to us for all the ways he screwed us over as kids."

Damien held up his hands. "Not happening. You know I don't accept anything from Dad. I'll take care of the bill."

"Do what you like, but I'm telling you, Dad has changed. He has a tough time getting past the ego to smooth things over with other people, but he wants to make things right with his sons. It's been…" Trey nod-ded thoughtfully for a moment, looking off into the distance while that pool water shimmered blue-pink behind him "…eye-opening to understand Dad better. And it's been even more of a wake-up call to realize he may have given us equal parts of his stubbornness. At least, it was for me."

Damien couldn't think through that mess of sticky family politics right now. Not with Miranda gone and potentially facing Rick Barrow alone. What the hell did that guy want from her?

"Let's wait and see on that one. For now, thanks for the extra security. I can't stand the idea of those vultures near her or near this place."

"Done. The bigger question is this—why haven't you gone after her yet?"

Damien pounded his fist on the granite in slow, rhythmic thunks, willing the right answer to come into his head. His eyes went to the refrigerator, where he knew the quiches she'd made were still stacked. He felt like a sap for wanting to open the appliance and stare at a bunch of tinfoil.

"I want to." It was killing him not to get in the truck and meet her at that hotel himself. "But I already told her I wanted her to stay. What can I say this time that's any different?"

"You can't think of anything you'd say differently? Any way you missed the point or didn't give her what she needed?" Trey leaned forward on the wide, cushioned pool lounger, staring into the webcam intently. "I'm telling you, dude, we were not raised with the kind of emotional sensitivity you might need in this situation."

"A week ago, I would have laughed my ass off at you for using phrases like 'emotional sensitivity.'" Damien wasn't laughing now. In fact, he prayed hard Trey had the answers he lacked. "But right now, I'm inclined to agree. I don't know what I'm doing and I don't know how to get her back."

"And that's what you want?"

More than any damn thing in the world. His chest ached as if someone had taken a baseball bat to it.

"She matters to me more than this farm, more than my debt to Ted and more than anything else that I thought was important before I met her."

"You have to tell her that." Trey stabbed his finger toward the camera. "That's the stuff she needs to know. How she's important and how much you care. Anything that you think is practical, like, logical reasons you belong together—I don't think that matters to women."

Damien remembered telling Miranda how much he wanted to keep her safe. Maybe that hadn't been the right approach. For that matter, he recalled how he'd sent her out the back window when the press arrived. That distinction—her going out the back alone while he talked to the media out front—had felt like a statement to Miranda. Maybe he should have walked out the front door with her. Put his arm around her during that press conference and made it clear she was off-limits, instead of sneaking her out the back.

Maybe he'd arranged the kind of escape he'd dreamed of as a kid instead of thinking about how Miranda wanted to handle it. He'd definitely never asked for her input.

"I don't know if anything I say is going to make a difference." Still, he stared at the tea and wondered if he could have told her how he felt. If he could have tried to put into words how much he cared about her already. How much more there could be for them.

"But you're a total stooge if you don't at least try. I'd even go so far as to say you might never forgive yourself if you don't try harder." Behind Trey, a pretty brunette with wide gray eyes approached the camera. She wore a pink bathrobe, her hair in a ponytail that lay on one shoulder. She waved into the camera even before Trey knew she was behind him.

Damien tried to find a smile for Courtney, but all he could think of was Miranda wearing his bathrobe this morning. Miranda smiling. Miranda twirling on the lawn and telling Violet Whiteman what a great place Fraser Farm was, and offering to make her tea.

"You're right, Trey." He needed to find her, tell her how he felt and keep telling her. "Thanks, man."

His brother wished him luck before disconnecting the call, Trey's eyes already on his fiancée and his future, while Damien sat alone in a kitchen that was way too big for one person. He just hoped it wasn't too late to tell Miranda that he wanted her back and it wasn't about keeping her safe. It was about building a life with her, since he couldn't imagine the days ahead—the years ahead—without her.

DAMIEN'S DRIVER PARKED MY SUV in the far corner of the lot behind the Sea Wind hotel after I left Fraser Farm, hoping to keep the vehicle out of the overhead lights in case the media knew what I was driving.

"I'll just walk you to the door." The driver, a young guy who'd been a particular fan of the Gruyère quiche, had been nice enough company for the ride over here. "You need anything from the back?"

"Yes." I started to open my door to retrieve it. "I'll grab it."

"Let me," he protested, levering open the driver side door. "What is it you need?"

"Floral print backpack. Lots of pins on it. It's hard to miss."

Bill grinned and passed me the car keys. "Sure thing."

I stuffed them in my purse and grabbed a few things from the console while Bill got the bag. No one had followed us from the farm. I felt sure of that, since I'd been in and out of Damien's house with lightning speed, eager to go before any reporters slowed my escape. If I didn't leave then, I might have been tempted to stay as he'd asked. And I knew that wouldn't be good for either of us.

Now I levered open the passenger door and hopped out.

"Do you see it?" I called, surprised Bill hadn't found it already.

True to the hotel name, sea wind coated my cheeks with damp, salty air as I moved toward the back of the vehicle.

"Bill?" A prickle of warning tripped over my senses even as I said the name.

Was it just me, or did the night seem unnaturally quiet?

"Hello, Shaelynn." A male voice sounded close to my right elbow.

I nearly leaped out of my skin. I hadn't heard that voice in person for six years, but I'd know it anywhere. I felt a cold, sick fear in my gut.

And why the *hell* had he just called me Shaelynn?

"Rick?" Turning, I found Nina's ex-husband beside me, his hands in the pockets of a denim jacket, where I couldn't see them.

I realized I was shaking, inside and out.

"Where's Bill?" I looked around wildly, scared.

"Down for the count, but definitely breathing." Rick pointed to a dark shadow on the ground. "Let's keep things quiet—you and me—to make sure he stays breathing. Okay?"

I went to scream, but only a hoarse croak emerged. It was like those dreams where you try to make a sound and nothing happens.

Rick noticed, though. He looped an arm around my neck and clamped a hand over my mouth. Pinning me to his side. Silencing me.

"Nice and quiet. Okay?" He smelled as if he hadn't washed in a week. Fear spread into cold, cold ice in my veins. I swallowed hard. Nodded. Hoped that Bill really was okay.

A million things ran through my brain. Unwashed and rumpled, Nina's ex-husband looked like crap. He'd aged in a lot of ways. Most ironic? After making me feel bad about myself for not being as svelte as my sister, Rick Barrow was now a stocky man. I pushed such crazy thoughts in the background for now and finally found enough of my voice to shout against the suffocating pressure of his palm. I tried to motion that I wanted to speak.

"Okay," he crooned in a soft, cajoling voice that made me want to throw up. "But quietly, or else I'll make sure your friend here doesn't wake up, okay? We don't want that on your conscience."

My stomach cramped harder. I nodded.

"How do you know about Shaelynn?" I blurted, when he finally moved his hand enough that I could speak. He kept me pinned to his side in a headlock, deep in the shadows behind the vehicle.

I didn't want to agitate him any more. His eyes gleamed with a crazy glint and he looked as if he was going to lose it any second. I was alone out here. Joelle didn't even know I'd come to crash in her hotel room for the night. I hadn't checked into the Sea Wind yet. And, in another stroke of brilliance, we'd parked as far away from the lobby as possible to hide from photographers.

My heart made a pitiful plea for Damien and all the safe, practical suggestions he would have offered if I'd stuck around the farm for another day.

"How do you think?" Rick thrust one hand into his pocket and I tried to edge farther from him, scared he might have a weapon. He must be seriously unstable if he'd tracked me down fifteen hundred miles from his home. But it wasn't a weapon he held up.

It was my flash drive.

He jerked me closer, cutting off circulation in my neck. When I started to choke, he loosened his hold a fraction.

"How did you get that?" I demanded, my eyes watering from the pressure at my throat.

"What do you mean, how did I get it? I took it right where you left it for me, in your computer." He smiled in a way that made me feel as if spiders were skittering over my skin. "When I followed you out of L.A. on Friday, I noticed you left the door to the SUV open for me when you abandoned the vehicle."

My brain hurried to process this. He'd followed me. He'd gone through my things.

"Rick, I didn't even know you were *in* L.A." The night air felt clammy on my skin and I swore I smelled desperation rolling off Rick along with the scent of cold sweat. "You do not have my permission to have that flash drive."

Maybe it was stupid to try and reason with him. But what else could I do? If there was any chance I could appeal to his rational side, maybe he'd let me go. Maybe he'd think we could be friends or something.

Damn it, who knew how he thought? I hadn't understood him six years ago and I sure as hell didn't understand him now.

He waved the flash drive in front of my nose again, but I refrained from batting at it like an uncoordinated kitten. I'd wait until I knew I could grab it. Besides, his hold on me loosened even more as he teased me.

"This is hot, Miranda. Really, really hot." He leered at me with brown eyes I'd once found handsome. Now I tried to hide a convulsive shudder, still hoping to get out of here without him…hurting me? I didn't know if that's what he had in mind, but I knew he'd manhandled me in the past when he'd gotten me into dark corners, even after his engagement to Nina.

There'd been a time I hadn't fought back, but those days were done. I'd grown stronger on my own, and then Damien had blasted away any lingering insecurities. I hadn't realized it until right this moment, but I was a far cry from the vulnerable woman Rick once knew.

"Rick, you're holding stolen property." I tried being reasonable, inching away from him a little at a time and hoping he wouldn't notice. "I suggest you return it before I press charges."

His eyebrows lifted. "I knew you'd gotten hotter over the years, but I didn't know you'd gotten fiery."

There was something foul in his tone. Something that scared me. My legs were shaking hard and I took another tiny step away, hoping I'd be able to run. He didn't know I was stronger now, and I could use that to my advantage—

"Where do you think you're going?" He grabbed me easily with one long arm and wrenched me back against him. "We've got business to discuss, Miranda."

I swallowed hard. I could still scream. Maybe I should have screamed already. But there were few opportunities and I was trying to bide my time for the right one. Also, I was so scared, I didn't trust my voice any more than my legs. For now, I was going to use the Nebraska Nice Girl skills. Maybe I'd take him by surprise as easily as I'd shocked the whole damn reality TV world.

*"Nice girls do not finish last!"* Shaelynn and I chorused silently together, giving rise to a near-hysterical giggle that I swallowed with a cough.

Oh, God, I was losing it. I probably wasn't thinking clearly after his chokehold had deprived my brain of oxygen a few minutes ago.

"State your business then, Rick. I've got a friend to

meet who is going to be looking for me if I don't get inside soon." I shivered from the breeze blowing off the Pacific, and the fact that Rick Barrow was holding on to me, his chili-dog breath making me gag and his sociopathic tendencies turning my belly to ice.

A set of headlights swung past us briefly and I prayed they'd come closer. Rick edged me farther behind the SUV. I listened hard and hoped the car had turned into the lot instead of continuing on Highway 1.

"You're done hanging out with farmer boy, for one thing," he breathed in my ear. "Whatever you thought you were doing with him is over, or else I'll go to the press with this erotic smut you've written, and embarrass the hell out of your Thoroughbred breeder with Shaelynn's porno adventures."

Anger growled to life inside me, vibrating in my ears and along the ground beneath me, giving me the push to find my voice.

"You son of a bitch." I shoved at him, hard, enough to loosen his hold. "How dare you—"

He bared his teeth like a rabid animal and cocked his arm back. I got ready to both scream and run like hell.

Except that his raised arm was suddenly wrenched backward so hard that Rick fell away from me, right into the waiting headlock of…Damien.

His handsome face appeared out of the night, his heavy biceps curled around Rick's face like a nutcracker ready to shell an almond. Rick deflated like the cowardly piece of crap he was, dropping my flash drive at my feet and launching into a tirade of whines.

"I didn't know she wanted it back," he protested, his

words muffled. "I thought she wanted me to read it. I was just going—"

The quick chirp of a siren and flash of police lights cut him off. I had a glimpse of his face reflected in red swirling light for a second before a squad car pulled up beside us. I scrambled over to Bill's side and checked his pulse. He was breathing just fine. Heartbeat steady, thank God. I realized now that Damien's Ford 450 idled nearby. That accounted for the growly, vibrating noise I'd heard earlier.

"You should pocket that," Damien said, pointing to the flash drive with his free hand.

Still watching out for me, even after I'd left him.

My heart hurt at the thought as I did what he'd suggested.

Before I could say anything to Damien—thank him for finding me and saving me—Joelle streaked across the parking lot in a white hotel robe, her normally perfect hair flying in every direction.

"Oh God, oh God, oh God, I nearly died when he grabbed you." Joelle swooped between me and one of two cops who'd arrived on the scene. The younger officer was helping Bill to sit up, while Joelle blurted, "Damien texted me to see if you were here, and I said no, but then I got worried and started looking out the window every now and then. When I saw your car and this guy, I called the cops, but they said they already had a car on the way, and I couldn't tell what was going on, but oh, God, I've been so scared."

Her words were fast and murmured into my shoulder while she hugged me. My heart still raced, adrenaline flowing through my veins and making me jittery. Or maybe it was the powerful emotions I felt for Damien, because all I really wanted to do right now was launch myself into his arms.

The cops had already helped Bill into the hotel for some water and a seat where it was warm. Another car arrived to take Rick away, the second set of officers ignoring his whining and protesting about whores and smut and Nebraska Backstabbers. I was pretty sure I'd be in the papers tomorrow even though I'd evaded the press at the farm. And I really regretted that.

"Thank you, Joelle." I hugged my friend tight and counted my blessings. I may have left my family in Nebraska six years ago, but I'd sure found an ally as strong as any blood tie in my former boss. "I'm so grateful."

"You can come back to work," she said between tears. "Maybe just take a few weeks off and all this will have died down. You can buy half my tearoom and we can run it together. I miss you, my friend."

"Wow." I wondered if the adrenaline had been at work for her, too, but that was still a really nice thing to offer. "That's very generous—"

"Miranda." Damien appeared beside us, pressing a palm on my shoulder and—oh, it felt so good—reaching for my hand. "Can we talk first? Privately?"

"We'll have some questions for her, Damien." One of the police officers spoke up. "Actually, we'll need a formal statement from you, too."

Damien nodded and Joelle pulled back, sniffling and clutching her cell phone. I noticed Damien's hand stayed on my shoulder, warm and strong. I wanted to curl into him with a fierceness that rocked me to my core, but I had to stay strong. I couldn't cave when times got tough. I wasn't the coward Rick had made me out to be, running from my problems.

This time, I really was running *toward* something. Strength, wholeness, fulfillment. Wherever I landed, back in L.A. or somewhere else, it would be my decision.

"Can we talk afterward?" Damien asked, his cheek close to mine.

I inhaled the scent of him. Leather and musk, horses and cinnamon tea. It seemed impossible we'd been in each other's arms just a few hours ago. It felt like a lifetime.

And no matter how difficult it might be to face him privately and not be swayed by the magnetic draw I felt whenever I was near him, I needed to at least say thank-you for what he'd done for me. He'd been right to worry about Rick. I shouldn't have been so careless.

"Of course." I tried to smile up at him, to prove to myself and to him that I was fine and strong and moving forward.

So it was really embarrassing that I chose that moment to burst into tears.

# _13_

DAMIEN LOOKED TO HIS FRIEND on the local cop squad, who gestured toward Miranda as if to say "she's all yours."

If only she was.

He'd barely shown up in time to help her, and then his request for a private audience made her cry. Damien would give his attempts to win her back a negative ten.

"Miranda?" It tore him up to hear those sobs wrenched from her throat. "Should we talk now? Just sit for a minute before the police take our statements? They can speak to Joelle first."

"No." Miranda shook her head, adamant. "I'm sorry. I'm fine. It's just been an emotional day."

His brother's words blared in his ears, about not being emotionally equipped to deal with romantic relationships. Damien was failing at this before he even started.

"Are you sure, miss?" The younger officer, a guy

with a nameplate that said Squire, approached Miranda. "This should only take a few minutes."

"I'm ready," she said. "I really have to tell you what a bastard that guy has been to me."

Damien wanted to hold her hand. Sit beside her while she told her story. But he'd been requested to make a statement, as well, since he'd had Barrow in a headlock when the police arrived. Besides, Miranda looked focused once she'd dried her tears. Something about the set to her shoulders told him she really *needed* to do this.

"She looks like she'll be okay," his friend Rafe assured him as he came over with a pad of paper and a pen in his hand. Rafe had been out to the farm more than once to ride his grandmother's horse, which boarded in Damien's stables, so they'd known each other awhile. "I wouldn't let him talk to her if she didn't seem ready, but my sense is the timing is good."

"I hope you're right." Damien tried to respect the other man's opinion, but it wasn't easy to squelch the urge to tuck her under his arm and take her away from this nightmare.

"Do you want to say anything formal about the so-called erotic novel that she was writing, or do you want to ignore that facet of Barrow's ranting?"

"Can I wait to see if Miranda wants to address that issue?"

Rafe grinned. "Mr. Fraser, I like to think we're friends, but when I'm on the job I can't let you match stories with your girlfriend."

"In that case, I will say that Miranda is a creative

force to be reckoned with, and she's working on a novel in addition to her acting career and her entrepreneurial efforts."

Rafe whistled as he transcribed the statement to his notebook. "Someone knows how to stick to the talking points."

"She's been through a lot, Rafe, and if I have my way she's going to be a valued member of this community for a long time. So it would mean a lot to me if we can treat her with as much respect as possible."

"Hey, my wife and I were rooting for the Nebraska Nice Girl the whole time." He looked up from his legal pad. "And yes, I recognized her. If someone was trying to hurt her tonight, we will prosecute to the full extent of the law."

The statement moved quickly after that. Damien tried to stick to the facts, though he got distracted a few times and glanced over at Miranda to be sure she was holding together. But she looked good. The officer who interviewed her appeared to take her seriously, writing copious notes as she spoke.

When Damien finished his interview, he walked Joelle back into the hotel and wished her a good night. By the time he returned to the parking lot, the officers were finishing up with Miranda. Once they left, Damien pointed toward his truck.

"It's warm in the cab. Do you mind if we talk in there, or would you rather go somewhere else?"

He didn't know if it was such a good idea to spend another second in the parking lot where Rick had grabbed her and threatened her, but Damien figured he'd let her make the call.

"That would be great, actually." She hugged herself. "I'm freezing."

He wasted no time opening the passenger door and helping her inside. When he'd settled into the driver's seat he reached behind him for a wool blanket and tucked it around her. It took superhuman effort not to wrap her in his arms, too. But he wanted to do this right. Couldn't allow himself to get lost in the taste of her to try and bridge the distance between them. If they were going to fix this, they needed to do it now, before she disappeared for good.

"Thank you," she blurted, before he could think where to start. "I don't know how you guessed where to find me, but thank God you did."

"I only wish I'd gotten here sooner—"

"I should have listened to you." She shook her head, gesturing with her sticker-covered fingernails. "It made sense to spend the night and come up with a better plan, but I didn't want to risk my heart another second, and I thought I'd better leave while I still could, and it was just…foolish."

He tried not to overthink the part about "risking her heart," but that sounded potentially hopeful, and he tucked it in a corner of his mind.

"I wasn't thinking clearly, either." He wanted to drink in the sight of her—whole and unharmed—for a few hours at least, until he reassured himself she was really okay. Safe. "I should have asked how you wanted to handle the onslaught of reporters, instead of calling all the shots and hiding you away like I wish I could have done back when it was me being hounded by the media."

"It was a good plan. I truly don't like facing that kind of mob scene." She took a tissue from a box between the two front seats and dabbed at her eyes.

"But I robbed you of the chance to meet them on your own terms. And maybe I could have spared you the encounter with Rick, too." That's what stung most. "If we'd stuck together—"

"Bottom line, I didn't want to draw more unwanted attention to Fraser Farm, and you helped me find a way to prevent that from happening, so I have no right to complain."

"You don't understand. I regret the way things happened because I don't care anymore about what effect your presence has on my business. I care about you more than I care about the public perception of the place."

She reached up to the ceiling and clicked on the overhead light. He blinked as his eyes adjusted to the brightness and to her scrutiny.

"What are you saying?" She squinted blue eyes at him as if trying to get a clearer picture.

"Miranda, I've lived like a hermit ever since I took on Fraser Farm. That's been by choice, because I don't trust easily."

"I can't blame you, after the craziness of those early dating years." She smoothed the fringe on the wool blanket he'd given her. "I haven't been in the habit of letting anyone get too close, either. But then, you can see why, after meeting the power-tripping lunatic who was my first relationship."

"Yet I wanted to reel you in and keep you close, starting that first day we met, and that's never happened to me before." The confession sounded rough. Felt rough, too. But he wanted her to stay, and not even a damned farm-stand sale was going to make it happen. If it took putting his heart on the line, he had every intention of doing just that. "When you looked at me and we shared that moment when Stretch first stood?" Damien smiled, remembering. "I knew then. I'd never want to let you go."

I HELD MY BREATH.

Actually, I held on to everything. My breath. The moment. The fringe in my hand. I guess I thought if I could stop time, I'd feel this happy forever.

Plus there wouldn't be any chance I'd misheard or misunderstood what this meant.

When I finally exhaled, I felt dizzy. Overwhelmed. But so full of hope I could burst.

"Do you mean—?"

"Please, don't go." Damien reached for my hand and held it. Then he reached for the other one and squeezed it, too. "Stay with me on the farm and do whatever you like. Run a tearoom. Ride horses. Write books. Bake quiches. Film a new reality show. Just...please be a part of my life."

I'm not the type to be tongue-tied. But this outpouring of unexpected...amazing...awesomeness was robbing me of speech at every turn. Plus, the more he talked, the more I liked what he was saying. The more I realized I wasn't dreaming. "You're serious."

"Everything comes alive when you're around. Me. The farm. My staff. My guests. It's like everything I've been working toward finally comes into focus when you're there. Without you, they're just pieces of the puzzle that don't quite fit." Damien looked out the windshield and I saw the first hint of self-doubt on his handsome, beloved face. "Help me out, Miranda. My brother said if I told you how I felt—"

I leaped into his lap. I hoped it wasn't painful, but I threw my arms around him and squeezed him tight. Kissed his gorgeous, chiseled features. Rained kisses down his temple. Tucked my head into his shoulder and cried. Happy tears, yes. But true to messy form, I blubbered and blathered and generally sobbed nonsense against his chest.

"I love being with you. I'm so happy at the farm. It's like home, but a million times better. Like the farm I always wanted and would have made for myself." I sniffled and he handed me tissues. Stroked my hair. I curled up until my butt was half through the steering wheel, but I didn't care. "Walking into your house was like Goldilocks going into the three bears' place, only better because nothing was too big or too small, everything was just right."

He laughed at that one, but I hope he knew what I meant.

"You'll stay?"

"Heck, yes, I'm staying! I'm going to put bonsai plants in all the windows and tea canisters all over the kitchen. Two days from now, you won't be able to picture that house without me in it, I promise you."

He *really* laughed at that one. But when he stopped, he clasped my face in his hands as if I was the most precious thing he'd ever held.

"I believe you and I can't wait."

My heart bloomed like a desert flower, as if it had been just waiting for him to treat it with this tender care. I felt happy from my toenails to my hair follicles and everywhere in between.

"I'm not sure we can keep the tabloids away." I fretted about this one last element. I so didn't want the drama of my life infringing on his. "But I know interest will fade...."

"I don't care about that." He crossed his heart with one finger. "I swear that doesn't matter anymore. When I made a big deal about that, it was a knee-jerk reaction from my past. But more media is going to be necessary to grow both sides of my business, and there are worse sorts of attention than what your fame can bring to the farm."

"I hope so."

He kissed all along my eyebrow, making me realize I must have the worried frown on my face that scrunched up my forehead. I relaxed and he continued speaking softly.

"I know so. Besides, no matter what kind of press you get, I want you. So that means we'll deal with it. Together."

"Wow." I marveled at him, this taciturn Sonoma County farmer who was sweeping me off my feet with all kinds of sweet talk. "I want to meet this brother of yours who got you to say all these things my heart was longing to hear."

"No way." His arm wrapped around my waist and he tugged me tighter. "Not until I'm convinced you're so far gone on me you could never look twice at anyone else."

"A jealous streak?" I kissed him, giddy with the idea that I could do that whenever I wanted from now on. "I'm learning so much about you, Damien. But you have no worries there, since I'm already halfway to loving you anyhow." In my heart, I knew that I did love him. Fiercely. But I was saving that tender admission for a night when I cooked for him and wore a cute dress and wasn't sprawled half across a pickup truck steering wheel. I liked thinking that we didn't have to rush things. That we could take our time getting to know each other and falling madly in love. "I'm just curious to meet your family. Plus, I want to know everything about you."

"I'm going to take such good care of you, Miranda Cortland." Damien's expression went all serious again and I felt a little awed to think his feelings for me were darn fierce, too.

I think I was only just beginning to understand what it might be like to be loved by a passionate, honorable, forever guy like Damien.

"I'm going to take such good care of you right back. You wait and see."

"Does that mean I get to take you home now?" He kissed my cheek and then captured my lips.

Our kiss was long, slow and deep. It left me breathless. It left me wanting. It left me anticipating every second of the future at his side.

"That means you can't drive fast enough for me," I teased, nipping his lower lip.

Gently, he settled me in the passenger seat, buckled me in and revved the engine.

"Just watch me." That flash of white teeth in the dim truck interior made me smile.

By the time we peeled out of the parking lot of the Sea Wind hotel, I was giggling with joy and the knowledge that I was going home with my Mr. Right and I was about to get very lucky.

Scratch that.

My luck had started right about the time my car broke down on Highway 1.

# *Epilogue*

*Six Months Later*

"Do you think it was a mistake to open on Wine Country Weekend?" Miranda asked for the tenth time, after she'd seated a third shift of afternoon tea patrons. "I'm so embarrassed to have people come for tea and not take a seat until six o'clock."

Tea Under the Oaks was packed with shoppers, diners and browsers, the crowd spilling out onto the porch and lawn, where gardens spread from the farm stand property well onto land that used to be Thoroughbred pasture. But since the tearoom was a joint holding, Damien didn't mind.

Actually, he'd tried to sell her that farm stand multiple times, to assure his fiancée that she would always have something that was just hers. But she didn't seem to need that kind of security. These days, she thrived like her gardens, her bonsai trees and everything else she touched.

"You wanted lots of traffic. You got it." Damien drew

her away from the hostess stand at the front of the tea-room, needing two minutes alone with her. "Come on. Stop for a minute and admire what you've done here, okay? Joelle can handle this. She's an old pro."

Miranda's friend winked at him as she stepped up to take over the role, only too glad to celebrate the grand opening of the tearoom. Patrons from Joelle's tearoom had made a trek, as if Tea Under the Oaks was some new mecca. Violet Whiteman had tweeted the details to her slew of followers, and tea drinkers from miles around responded to the call. Trey's wife, Courtney, had brought some friends from the wealth management firm where she worked, too.

In fact, Miranda had so many supporters through friends and family, she hardly had room for the huge influx of Sonoma County tourists on Wine Country Weekend.

"How can I leave when I have so much to do?" she protested, but walked with him, chattering nervously, waving to newcomers and making kissy-faces at babies held by a few customers wandering around out front.

"You don't want to miss this, trust me." Damien kept walking until he had her perfectly positioned, centered in front of the lawn. Then he turned her so she could face her creation. "You see?" He pointed up at the build-ing, which was painted, primped and decked out ex-actly as she'd imagined. "It looks just like the picture you drew."

Right down to the banner flapping in a lazy sum-mer breeze.

"Only now there are people in it." She sighed and

leaned into him, her head fitting comfortably against his shoulder. "It's perfect, isn't it?"

"You're perfect," he argued, kissing her hair—blond these days, with streaks of pink or baby blue, depending on her mood. Depending on whether she thought she was carrying a girl or a boy, their first baby.

She wasn't due for seven months, but she was already planning and dreaming. Damien wondered if any of her friends understood what those streaks in her hair meant.

He liked being able to read her moods. Liked being able to see the changes she made to their house and the farm every day. And he really, really liked helping her work on her erotic novel.

"It won't be this busy every day," she told him suddenly, reaching up to kiss his cheek. "Once things are running smoothly, I'll hire more help."

"That's good. I don't want you getting tired out." He nodded at a few potential Thoroughbred buyers who'd stopped in the tearoom.

The buyers—investors from Kentucky—were excited about two stallions and were willing to pay a very healthy price for them. Business was good.

"You keep saying I'm going to be tired, but I feel better than ever." She did a twirl to prove it, an impromptu dance move that made her print skirt swirl out and her curls bounce around her cheeks. "See? Full of energy."

"Excellent. That means you'll be able to go to Town Hall with me tonight and make things official." He picked up her left hand and kissed the backs of her fingers near the princess-cut diamond he'd placed there four months after declaring his undying devotion, his love and his need to publicly claim her as his wife.

He would never forget the feeling he'd had when she said yes. Whatever else he achieved in life, it wouldn't compare to that. Although, maybe seven months from now, he'd feel differently.

He rubbed a hand over her still-flat belly while a few horses trotted past on the exercise track that ran behind the tearoom.

"Town Hall... I guess we could do that." She gave a careless shrug and a wink, less concerned than him about finalizing the deal she said was already signed, sealed and delivered in her heart. "Or maybe you should stay at home and see what naughty adventures Shae-lynn has been having...."

"You've been writing again?" He'd never get her to Town Hall at this rate, damn it. His blood was already simmering just thinking about how daring Miranda's alter ego had gotten lately.

"Yes. I'm telling you, pregnancy agrees with me. I've never felt so creative and full of energy."

He kissed her cheek and squeezed her shoulders, so proud of her for her triumphant grand opening and all she'd achieved here. She had decided the naughty novel was just for them and just for fun, but she'd devoted time to the horse rehab efforts, taking a training course and reading books on working with Thoroughbreds. Of course, that was on hiatus while she was expecting, but even now, she used her Nebraska Nice Girl fame to draw attention to the Thoroughbreds who needed another chance in life.

"Perfect. We'll say the vows, sign the papers and still have time to read your latest chapter," he teased.

Miranda studied him for a long moment, four silver earrings winking in the sunlight. "That sounds great."

"It does?" He nearly choked on the words, he was so damn surprised.

"Yes! I said I'd marry you, Damien Fraser. Did you think I wouldn't?" She put her arms around his shoulders and hugged him hard. "I love you with all my heart, you gorgeous, smooth-talking Casanova. I'm dying to be your wife. I've just been busy getting the tearoom together. But now that I see this—" she gestured with one arm spread wide "—it all feels right and perfect. I'd love to marry you tonight and celebrate our happily ever after."

"You don't think it's wrong that we're not inviting anyone else?" He felt a twinge of guilt about that. "I don't want you to think you can't have a big, fairy-tale wedding. There's still time—"

"We'll have a party another time and invite our friends, but we're not the kind of couple who needs a big hoopla, right?" She'd said the same thing to him before, often enough that he believed it. She never would be close with her family, and while he'd mended fences with his, he didn't mind celebrating his marriage to Miranda privately.

"I'm fine with it, but I want you to be happy. I don't want you to ever have any regrets about our wedding."

"Never." She shook her head. "Besides, I've already got the fairy tale." She threaded her fingers through his and locked their hands together. "Right here with me every day. All the time."

Damien kissed her, mentally adding to the vows he had planned. He loved her, honored her...yes. But he was also going to make her the happiest woman on earth, since she'd already made all his dreams come true.

* * * * *

# COMING NEXT MONTH FROM

## Available January 21, 2014

### #783 A SEAL's SALVATION
*Uniformly Hot!*
by Tawny Weber
Good girl Genna Reilly saved Brody Lane once when her attempted seduction got him shanghaied into the Navy. Can her love save this sexy SEAL again, now that his world is falling apart?

### #784 TEXAS OUTLAWS: BILLY
*The Texas Outlaws*
by Kimberly Raye
Rodeo cowboy Billy Chisholm wants one hot night of wild, unforgettable sex. Unfortunately, he gets more than he bargains for when he meets Sabrina Collins, who not only gets into his head, but finds a place in his heart.

### #785 GAME ON
*Last Bachelor Standing*
by Nancy Warren
Adam Shawnigan is sexy, single...and in serious trouble when performance coach Serena Long is hired to improve his hockey skills. Now there's another game in play—and Adam's bachelorhood is in jeopardy!

### #786 HARD TO HOLD
*The U.S. Marshals*
by Karen Foley
Reformed con artist Maddie Howe must revert to her former ways in order to rescue her brother, even if it means kidnapping the hunky U.S. marshal who is hot on her trail!

---

**YOU CAN FIND MORE INFORMATION ON UPCOMING HARLEQUIN® TITLES, FREE EXCERPTS AND MORE AT WWW.HARLEQUIN.COM.**

HBCNM0114

# REQUEST YOUR FREE BOOKS!
## 2 FREE NOVELS PLUS 2 FREE GIFTS!

### HARLEQUIN®
### *Blaze®*
### red-hot reads!

# A SEAL's Salvation

by Tawny Weber

*It all began ten years ago….*

"Genna, you're crazy. You don't have to do this."

"Of course I do. You dared me." Genna Reilly gave her best friend a wide-eyed look.

She needed to do this. Now, while anticipation was still zinging through her system, making her feel brave enough to take on the world. Or, in this case, to take down the sexiest bad boy of Bedford, California.

She wanted Brody Lane.

But he had practically made a career of ignoring her existence.

Time to end that.

So tonight, thanks to Dina's dare, she was going to do something about it.

"I don't kiss and tell," Genna murmured.

"You mean you don't kiss or do anything else," Dina corrected, rolling her eyes.

"The dare was to kiss Brody Lane," Sylvie pointed out, glancing nervously toward the garage. "Genna's not going in there unless she follows through."

Genna looked toward the garage, the silhouette of a man working on a motorcycle.

"If I'm not back in ten minutes, head home," she instructed, fluffing her hair and hurrying off.

Carefully she peeked around the open doorway.

There he was. Brody Lane, in all his bare-chested glory. Black hair fell across his eyes as he bent over the Harley. She had the perfect view of his sexy denim-clad butt.

Genna fanned herself. Oh, baby, he was so hot.

She took a deep breath, then stepped through the doorway.

And waited.

Nothing.

"Hey, Brody," she called out, her voice shaking slightly. "How're you doing?"

His body went still, his head turned. His eyes, golden-brown like a cat's, narrowed.

Slowly, he straightened away from the bike, the light glinting off that sleek golden skin. Her gaze traveled from the broad stretch of his shoulders down his tapered waist to his jeans, slung low and loose on his hips.

Oh, wow.

"Genna?" He cast a glance behind her, then back with an arched brow. "What the hell do you want?"

**Pick up A SEAL'S SALVATION**
**by Tawny Weber, available wherever you buy**
**Harlequin® Blaze® books.**

# The stakes are high!

Reformed con artist Maddie Howe must revert to her former ways in order to rescue her brother, even if it means kidnapping the hunky U.S. marshal who is hot on her trail! From the Sierra Nevada foothills to the glittering casinos of Reno, Colton Black will go along as her "hostage" in order to keep her safe, even at the risk of losing his badge—and his heart.

Don't miss

## *Hard to Hold*

by *Karen Foley,*
available this February wherever you buy
Harlequin Blaze books.